Old Testament
Albert Smith's Mystery Thrillers Book 4
Steve Higgs

Text Copyright © 2025 Steve Higgs

Publisher: Steve Higgs

The right of Steve Higgs to be identified as author of the Work has been asserted by him in accordance with the Copyright, Designs and Patents Act 1988

All rights reserved.

The book is copyright material and must not be copied, reproduced, transferred, distributed, leased, licensed or publicly performed or used in any way except as specifically permitted in writing by the publishers, as allowed under the terms and conditions under which it was purchased or as strictly permitted by applicable copyright law. Any unauthorised distribution or use of this text may be a direct infringement of the author's and publisher's rights and those responsible may be liable in law accordingly.

'Old Testament' is a work of fiction. Names, characters, businesses, organisations, places, events, and incidents either are the product of the author's imagination or are used fictitiously. Any resemblance to actual persons, living, dead or undead, events or locations is entirely coincidental.

Contents

1. Chapter 1 — 1
2. Chapter 2 — 7
3. Chapter 3 — 14
4. Chapter 4 — 19
5. Chapter 5 — 24
6. Chapter 6 — 30
7. Chapter 7 — 37
8. Chapter 8 — 39
9. Chapter 9 — 45
10. Chapter 10 — 49
11. Chapter 11 — 53
12. Chapter 12 — 59
13. Chapter 13 — 65
14. Chapter 14 — 69
15. Chapter 15 — 75
16. Chapter 16 — 82
17. Chapter 17 — 91
18. Chapter 18 — 96

19.	Chapter 19	103
20.	Chapter 20	105
21.	Chapter 21	110
22.	Chapter 22	115
23.	Chapter 23	118
24.	Chapter 24	122
25.	Chapter 25	129
26.	Chapter 26	133
27.	Chapter 27	137
28.	Chapter 28	142
29.	Chapter 29	146
30.	Chapter 30	152
31.	Chapter 31	161
32.	Chapter 32	165
33.	Chapter 33	169
34.	Chapter 34	172
35.	Chapter 35	176
36.	Chapter 36	181
37.	Chapter 37	183
38.	Chapter 38	185
39.	Chapter 39	188
40.	Chapter 40	190
41.	Epilogue	194
42.	Author notes:	196

43.	History of the dish:	199
44.	What's Next for Albert and Rex?	201
45.	Free Books and More	202

Chapter 1

The train was on time, but where that might have been the first line of a joke in England, it was completely normal in Germany. Even thinking it, Albert knew he was being a little unfair, rail services in the UK had improved vastly since privatisation in the nineties.

Regardless, the train was approaching the platform just as the clock ticked around to 1203hrs.

"Ready, Rex?" he asked.

His human was acting oddly. Displaying an unusual and as yet unexplained sense of anticipation Rex could not fathom. They rode trains every few days to get from one place to the next. What was special about this one?

Albert had his backpack on. It forced him to sit forward in his chair, which was a little uncomfortable, but they were about to get off, so it really didn't matter. His small, blue suitcase was in his left hand, and he had Rex's lead gripped firmly in his right. Looking out through the window, he strained his eyes to find familiar faces.

Wing Commander (retired) Roy Hope and his wife, Beverly, were meeting him at the station and had already texted to say they were on the platform waiting. His friends were also his neighbours, a couple who had lived across the street for decades. They were of a similar age and when his wife was alive, they went out as a foursome.

After losing Petunia more than a year ago, things changed as they inevitably had to, but he still saw the folks across the street on a regular basis. They were in Europe for a nostalgic tour around some of the places they became familiar with during Roy's time in the Royal Air Force.

He spent more than twenty years at different bases in Germany, one of which was the nearby RAF Hoffenholen. Sitting just across the border from the Netherlands, it was closed in the late nineties, but according to some of Roy's old comrades, apart from the gates closing, from the outside at least, it looked as though very little had changed.

Albert had, of course, never seen the place, but one location was as good as any other and he'd discovered a love for exploring that started a few months ago on the anniversary of his wife's passing. That trip took him around the British Isles, but in an unexpected quirk of fate, his adventures made his face one that people across the UK would recognise, so it was as much to escape the constant selfies and questions that he chose the European mainland for his second expedition.

Spotting first Beverly and then Roy, Albert tried waving to get their attention. Of slight build, Roy sported an impressive handlebar moustache. It was pure white to match his full head of hair. It made Albert a little jealous since he could count the hairs on his head without needing to employ both hands. Thin red lines encircled Roy's face like a map of the London Underground, and he wore a smart navy-blue blazer beneath a thick winter coat. In his right hand he carried a thin walking cane.

Two years his junior, Beverly was a little thicker at the hips than she had been in her youth, but her bust had grown too as if noting the need to keep her figure in balance. Wearing her hair shoulder length, it was dyed with multiple tones to make it a lustrous light brown that somehow looked natural despite her advancing years. Bedecked in winter clothes and sturdy boots, she looked ready for adventure.

Albert stopped waving his hand when he realised they couldn't see him. Passengers were spilling from the train, and he was far from the fastest to step down to the platform. Both his neighbours were craning their heads and standing on tiptoes to see if they could spot him, but it wasn't until Albert told Rex to bark that they angled their heads his way.

Rex had no idea why the old man wanted him to speak. Perhaps it was to clear the crowded platform of people pressing in around them. Which is precisely what happened.

The loud noise made multiple people jump and a little girl wailed when the 'bad dog' startled her. Rex offered to lick her chin to prove he wasn't going to hurt anyone, but by then the little lady's mother was tugging her away while glaring at the old man holding Rex's lead.

"Albert, old boy!" hallooed Roy, snaking through the crowd with Beverly holding his hand and trying to keep up. He raised his cane to make sure he could be seen.

Thankful to see they looked as healthy and happy as ever, Albert put his case down and swapped the dog lead out of his right hand so he could greet his friends.

Rex's ears pricked up when he heard a familiar voice call his human's name. Sniffing deeply, his tail began to wag.

"*Hey, that's Roy and Beverly!*" His paws bounced with excitement. He loved humans for their company and not just because they have food. The neighbours from across the street were fun people to be around and always made a big fuss of him.

"Roy!" Albert slapped his hand into Roy's.

"Albert!"

"Beverly!" Albert released Roy's hand so he could hug his friend's wife.

"Good to see you, Albert," she kissed his cheek.

Releasing her, Albert asked, "Have you been waiting long?"

Frowning, Rex barked, "*Hey! Aren't you all forgetting someone?*"

Laughing, Albert ruffled the fur on Rex's head and stepped aside so he could become the centre of attention.

Lapping up the ear scratches and general praise, Rex basked in the wonder of human adoration.

"Well, no sense hanging around here at the train station," said Albert as he clicked his tongue to get Rex moving. "Shall we head out?"

"Indeed," Roy agreed, falling into step beside his friend. "We only got here half an hour ago. Long enough to grab a coffee, but no more than that. We're rather hoping to see if an old schnellie we used to visit is still there and ..."

Albert interrupted, to ask, "What's a schnellie?"

Roy blinked. Then he looked at Beverly. "Oh, er, it's the word for a fast-food place. There's one in every town. Normally, they are just a hole in the wall with a kitchen on the other side, but some places have a few chairs and table inside, and this one is like that. What was the name of it, darling?"

"Treffenplatz," Beverly supplied without needing to think. "Of course that was more than twenty years ago. If it's still there and hasn't turned into a Domino's Pizza, it might easily be called something else now, anyway."

"A schnellie," Albert tried the word out. "I shall remember that." He'd learned a little German in school and refreshed his knowledge when his kids found it on their curriculum, but he was a long way from being able to hold a conversation.

"Anyway," Roy continued, "it's not lunchtime yet and we figured you would want to take Rex for a walk so we thought we might check out an old jogging route we used to take through the woods by the base."

Albert nodded appreciatively. "Sounds good."

Rex heard the word 'walk' but he was already outside. His nose filtered the cool winter air, idly sampling it for anything interesting. He could smell discarded sushi that was probably coming from a bin to his left, and a strong whiff of coffee fought to dominate all other scents. There were rats around; he could smell their droppings, and somewhere ahead of him walked a man in need of a shower.

"The car is in the car park," Beverly pointed the way. "The base is about a ten-minute drive from here."

Albert expected that she was underestimating, but her prediction was on the money. On the back seat of her BMW, with Rex stretched out and his head on Albert's lap, he looked through the window at the imposing fence he could see through the trees to his right.

"That's the base?"

Roy stared at it too. "Yes. That's RAF Hoffenholen. Not that they call it that anymore, I'm sure."

"It's closed down though, right?"

"You're asking why the fence is still there thirty years later? I don't have an answer to that, but my guess would be that the old girl was repurposed for something else. In the UK old bases have been bought by commercial operations. The real estate has value, as do the buildings. Ah, here we are."

Beverly flicked on her indicator and pulled off the road and down a short path running parallel with the fence. It was a secluded spot, hidden from sight on all sides except the rear, but to see them from that angle, a car would have to drive in behind them.

"We've parked in this exact spot more times than I care to recall."

"Especially in the early days just before we were married, eh?" Roy nudged his wife's arm and grinned cheekily.

Beverly blushed and shot daggers with her eyes.

Albert pretended not to notice and opened his door to get out.

"Come along, Rex," he called to drown out the dressing down Roy was getting from Beverly who hissed annoyed whispers in his direction.

Rex bounced out of the car, across the dirt and onto the scrubby grass where he immediately found an old log on which to relieve himself. They were going for a stroll through the woods and that suited him just fine. There would be rabbits to chase and squirrels to avoid.

Albert called him back before he could get too far but pleasingly showed no sign of wanting to connect his collar to the lead.

Once the other humans were out of the car they set off down a path between the trees. The undergrowth was sparse, the summer growth dying back to reveal the routes small animals took under the foliage to keep out of sight. Rex sniffed them all, revelling in the opportunity to explore.

The humans talked, chatting amiably and both Roy and Beverly reminisced about their time living in and around the base until Albert held up a hand to stop them.

"Did you hear that?" he asked.

Rex turned toward the fence. "*I did.*" His ears were up, and his nose was searching.

"Didn't hear a thing, old boy," said Roy, following Albert's gaze.

Their route through the woods took them alongside the fence in places and right now they were just a few yards from it. At two and a half yards high with barbed wire along the top, it looked old, but convincing enough to deter all but the most determined intruders. The final two feet of barbed wire canted out at forty-five degrees to make clambering up and over from the outside all but impossible.

A dog barked in the distance. It was followed by the same from a second animal and Albert had heard enough barks in his time to know these two were the vicious kind.

"*They're chasing someone,*" said Rex, his feet taking him unbidden to the edge of the fence.

It was the someone that had caught Albert's attention. He couldn't calculate how far away she was, but the distant wail of a woman, many might not have even noticed, had registered an alert in his brain. She was in trouble. He couldn't express how he knew it, but there was no doubt in his mind.

Chapter 2

"What is it, Albert?" Beverly wanted to know. She had been speaking and missed the woman's cry. It was yet to be repeated, so all she could hear was some dogs barking in the distance.

Albert didn't reply. Not yet. He wasn't sure if it was anything at all, or what he could do if it was. The sound very definitely came from the other side of the fence and there was no way that he could see to get through it.

However, when the terrified cry of a woman disturbed the near silent sanctity of the woods a moment later, there was no mistaking it, and this time Roy and Beverly heard it too.

Squinting through the trees, Albert pointed with his right arm. "Roy, can you check that way? See if there is a break in the fence anywhere."

"Righto."

Albert gripped the fence and gave it a shake. It was quite solid.

"Do you think she might be in trouble?" asked Beverly.

Albert was about to answer when the sound of the dogs barking was joined by the distant whine of motorbike engines. It came from a long way off but was getting closer.

"Can you shout, please, Beverly? I think it would do for whoever that is to hear a woman's voice." Albert didn't know if it would make any difference, but he knew from years of bitter experience as a police detective that almost all women in distress were happier to see another woman than a man.

Beverly cupped her hands around her mouth. "Hey! Over here! Hello! Do you need help?"

"That's perfect," said Albert, moving around her to see if he could spot the woman if he changed positions. "Keep going."

With Beverly calling for the unknown person to come toward her voice, Albert continued to adjust his position. The trees were not what he would call dense, and the undergrowth was all but gone, but he still couldn't see more than a few yards because thick brambles coated the ground.

He called to Roy, "Anything?"

Roy's voice floated back, "Not yet, old boy. Fence looks as good as it did the last time I saw it."

Rex barked, excited to get involved and was about to bark again when Albert clamped a hand over his muzzle.

Coming down to his level, he said, "I need you to keep quiet, Rex. I'm not sure what we are witness to, but I'm rather worried that woman is being chased by the dogs we can hear."

"*Yes!*" Rex tried to reply, his barks coming out very muffled with his human's hands keeping his mouth shut. "*That's precisely what is happening!*" It often surprised Rex just how intuitive the old man could be.

The woman, the dogs, and the motorbikes were all coming closer, the sound from each increasing in volume with each passing second.

Beverly shouted, "Over here!" and "Come this way!" for the eighth or ninth time and finally got a reply.

"Help!" The cry came in accented English. It belonged, Albert judged, to a young woman. She was out of breath and very scared. "Help me! I'm being chased!" A sharp cry of pain followed her request and then some words in a different language. Albert didn't understand them, but the tone she employed made him believe he was hearing the young woman curse.

Rex paced the fence, keeping quiet only because his human asked him to. He felt tense and his hackles were raised. There were dogs coming and he could hear the excitement in their barks. Blocked by the fence, he wanted to intervene, and it frustrated him that he couldn't do anything to help.

Beverly shouted, "Keep coming!" and squinted to see through the trees. At a more normal volume, she said, "I think I can see her," and pointed through the fence.

"Yes," Albert murmured, "I see her too."

The motorbikes were closing fast, and the dogs couldn't be far behind her. It was a race that was going to end when the woman reached the fence. She would be trapped against it. Unable to go through, she would be forced to choose left or right, but there was no sign of a break anywhere.

Frantically, Albert demanded his brain supply a solution. The angled barbed wire portion at the top of the fence made climbing it impossible, but staring up at the ugly barbs, Albert saw his mistake. The fence was designed to keep people out. The angled section at the top wasn't replicated on the inside, so a person trying to get out could reach the top and roll over. They would sustain cuts and scratches, but the injuries to be endured would seem like nothing by comparison to what might otherwise occur.

Bursting into sight, the woman swiped a small branch aside with an arm and leapt an old log. Her long brunette hair flowed behind her like a flag in a stiff breeze. There were bits of leaf litter in it and mud stained her lower legs and the dress she wore. Her arms were bare, as were her feet, and the dress was the only garment she wore.

Thinking she had to be freezing in the frigid winter air, Albert saw blood on her arms and her face. They were from multiple deep scratches, most likely where thorny plants caught her skin as she fled whatever terror she sought to escape.

Joining Beverly, he called, "Over here! You can climb the fence!"

The woman flicked her eyes in his direction, letting him see the fear they held, and she altered her angle to run directly at him.

She looked exhausted. Each breath was a ragged gulp of air that failed to replenish her body's demands for oxygen. Seeing her confirmed everything Albert feared. Only a person fearing for their life would run as she was.

"There's the dogs!" cried Beverly, her own voice betraying the fear she now felt for the running woman. "Quickly! Hurry!"

Roy joined in, shouting encouragement, but Albert could see she wasn't going to make it. The distance between her and the fence was too great. The dogs would get to her first. There was no question.

The dogs were a pair of Dobermanns. Their sleek, muscular frames ate up the ground at ten times the speed the woman could manage. In two seconds they would be upon her.

"*Hey!*" barked Rex, snarling and baring his teeth. It was enough to snatch their attention away from the woman's fleeing legs, but only for the briefest of moments.

His heart beating dangerously fast, Albert wanted to tear the fence apart, but as he held his breath, unable to tear his eyes away from the terrible scene about to unfold, the woman shocked him.

Young, lean, and lithe, she leapt into the air, grabbed a low hanging branch and used her forward momentum to swing herself up and onto it. Almost upon her, the Dobermanns couldn't change their course fast enough when she vanished into the air above their heads.

They skidded to a stop in the dirt and fallen leaves, but by then the woman was making her way along the branch to get to the trunk.

Barking through the fence, Rex demanded, "*What are you doing? Is she a criminal? Why are you chasing her?*"

His questions went ignored as the brutish dogs snapped, leapt, and barked at the woman.

"That's it," Albert called to her. "Keep coming! You can make it!"

He'd not considered it, but there were branches crossing over the top of the fence from both sides. He'd thought she might clamber up the fence and escape over the top of the barbed wire, but she was going to avoid it entirely.

The motorbikes were closing in, the sound from the engines telling Albert and his friends there were no more than a few seconds before they came into sight.

It turned out to be less than that.

Two dirt bikes, one bright red, the other yellow, exploded through the trees at a speed that had to be dangerous to maintain.

In the tree, the woman used another branch above her head to keep her balance as she edged farther and farther out from the trunk. The branch bowed under her weight, and she almost slipped.

Unable to do anything to help, Albert could only watch and pray, his attention divided between the woman above his head and the oncoming motorcycles.

The dirt bikes were ridden by men. Their helmets obscured their features, but they were both trim and muscular. Gunning their throttles, they came straight for the fence, skidding to a stop just when the woman decided she was far enough out to make the jump.

The bowing branch had stopped when it met the top of the fence. It meant she had enough support to drop down and grab the branch in her hands. Hanging from it, she dropped lightly to the ground where Albert made sure she didn't fall. The moment she had her balance, he handed her off to Beverly and used his body as a physical barrier between her and the men on the motorbikes.

They flicked their visors up but did not remove their helmets.

"Mila. This is stupid," one warned, his voice a growling threat. "Stay where you are, and we will come to get you."

Albert stepped forward so his face was almost pressing against the fence. It brought him within half a yard of the man who'd spoken. Roy came to stand beside him.

"What is this?" Albert demanded. "Why are you chasing her?"

"Stay out of this, old man. She belongs with us. Getting involved will only result in trouble you don't want."

"Oh?" said Roy. "But we rather like trouble. Don't we, Albert?"

Albert didn't get a chance to answer because the woman was getting her breath back and had things she wanted to say. Not that she said them exactly.

"You pigs!" she spat. "You're all filthy lying pigs! You were never going to let me see my sister!" Much to Albert's surprise she then actually spat through the fence, a glob of spittle landing on the nearest man's leather jacket.

He didn't even bother to look down at it.

"Mila, no one is stopping you from seeing your sister. You're just not ready yet, and you know that already. She came to us, yet you act as though we are keeping her prisoner."

"Liar! You're a liar, Bruno!"

Beverly had taken off her coat and was trying to put it around the younger woman.

"Mila, put this on. You are freezing."

"That's because these pigs took all my belongings."

Bruno continued to argue, "Mila, you know better than that. Attachment to the material is detachment from the spiritual."

Mila took the coat with a nod of thanks and began to back away. "Do you have a car?" she asked, letting Beverly place a guiding arm around her shoulders. "They will send more. I need to get away from here."

Albert had only the vaguest idea what trouble he'd walked into, but one thing was clear: the woman needed his help.

Just along the fence, Rex was growling at the two Dobermanns. They had their faces up against the fence and were snarling threats in return.

"*You're lucky this fence is in the way, little shepherd dog,*" growled the first. "*Cerberus and I eat pieces of crap like you for breakfast.*"

Rex twitched one eyebrow. "*You eat pieces of crap for breakfast? That doesn't sound particularly nutritious. I prefer kibble for my morning meal ...*"

"*No, that's not what Hades meant,*" snapped Cerberus.

"*It's what he said.*"

"*Yeah, well, you're stupid,*" replied Hades, trying to get back on top.

"Says the one eating crap for breakfast."

"That's not what I meant!" Hades barked.

Rex shrugged. *"It would explain why your breath is so bad."*

Albert called, "Rex. It's time to go."

Rex turned his head to check what his human was doing. The young woman was with Beverly and the whole party was moving away, heading back the way they had come from the car. He took a moment to deliver a more serious line.

"If I see you again, boys, you'd better hope this fence is still between us. You don't get to hurt humans. Not on my watch." He turned away, paying no heed to the threats that followed his tail when he jogged to catch up with the humans.

"Mila!" shouted Bruno, now off his dirt bike to follow her along the fence line. "How far do you think you will get? What about Talia, Mila?" When she offered no response other than a quick glance over her shoulder, he ran back to his bike. Moments later both bikes roared away.

Mila said, "We should hurry. They will send people to find us outside the fence."

Unable to contain herself any longer, Beverly asked, "What kind of trouble are you in Mila? Who were those men? Why are they after you?"

"Just get me away from here, please," Mila begged. "I will tell you everything as soon as we are somewhere safer."

Chapter 3

The trio of pensioners made their best speed to get back to the car with Mila. Rex danced along at Albert's side, unsure what was happening, but excited to be out doing something fun.

They needed to move fast, not just because of Mila's warnings, but due to her condition. Half frozen from the cold, her feet were white and numb. Adrenaline and physical exertion had kept her warm, but the moment she dropped to the ground outside the fence, the spent adrenaline left her system. Now exhausted, Roy and Beverly were buoying her along between them.

"It's not much farther," Roy told her for the third time.

Thankfully, it really wasn't, and the relief of shutting the cold air outside was eclipsed only when the fans pushed warm air into the car.

Still shivering, her lips blue, Mila said, "We should get moving. It would be bad for them to see your car."

Beverly started the engine and wasted no time turning around to go back the way they came.

"Where do I go?" she asked.

"Our accommodation," said Albert. Sitting on the back seat, he had Rex between him and Roy. Mila was in the front where the heated seat could help to warm her body.

"What about the police?" asked Beverly. "Shouldn't we take her there?"

"NO!" Mila's response cut through the car like a bullet. "No. Please. No police."

Albert chewed on his lip. The men who chased her were not overtly threatening. They spoke calmly, almost begging her to see sense and return to them, but there was something off about the fence and Mila's desperate need to get away. Thinking there could be dozens of explanations for her flight, none of them made sense if she wanted to hide from the police. Unless …

"Are you here, illegally, Mila?" Her accent wasn't German.

Mila's eyes were already locked on the carpet and her voice was quiet when she admitted, "Yes. I have no visa to stay in this country. That's not the real problem, though."

"So what is?" asked Beverly, flicking her eyes across to their unexpected passenger.

Mila shuddered. The warm air was beginning to thaw her out, but the cold was in her bones, and she was going to need a while to feel normal again.

"That place … I went there voluntarily. No crime has been committed. Not that I can attest to at least. There's nothing to report to the police."

"Why were you trying to escape then?" asked Beverly, pressing to understand what was going on. "Did they hurt you?"

"No," Mila replied, her voice quiet. "They didn't hurt me."

Silence fell, each of the car's occupants keeping their own thoughts until Albert recalled something Bruno said.

"Who's Talia?"

Mila lifted her head and twisted in her seat to look at Albert. There was a tear in her eye when she said, "My sister. She's still at the camp." She turned back to face the direction of travel but continued to talk. "I mean, I think she's at the camp. They wouldn't let me see her. They kept saying I wasn't ready yet. I needed to find my inner peace first and only then, when I had thrown off the ties that prevented my spiritual growth, would I be allowed access to the community where I believe she is staying."

Absorbing what she said and how she said it, Albert asked, "Is it a cult?"

Mila gave a slow shrug. "Maybe. A cult, a community … different people would give it different names, but they call it a spiritual retreat. Horst talks of harmony with the world, of throwing off that which binds our lives and prevents true freedom. In practice, I believe they seduced my sister into joining them and now they won't let her go. Then there is something Horst calls digital ascension. It's part of the journey to finding true happiness. If I wanted to see my sister, I had to surrender myself to their way of thinking and that included handing over my identity."

"Digital ascension?" Albert repeated the odd term.

"Yes. It's the process of disconnecting ourselves from the 21st century. Phone, devices, computers … residents going into Unlimited Horizons must give all that up if they want to enter. They hand over their bank cards and identification, essentially become a non-person."

"So why were you trying to escape?" Albert pushed her to explain. He thought the place sounded terrible and questioned whether any person in their right mind would entertain their rules, but Mila said she went inside willingly to find her sister.

"Because it's all a lie. They wouldn't let me see my sister. For all I know they've done something to her."

"Surely that means we need to go to the police," Beverly repeated her earlier suggestion.

Albert said, "If people willingly hand over their wealth, there is no crime. Mila is right that there is nothing to investigate."

"But they wouldn't let her see her sister. They were trying to stop Mila from leaving." Beverly protested.

"Yes, but that's not against the law. We would have to prove Talia is being held against her will. To do that would require a warrant to search the premises and find her. Obtaining that would be a long and rather drawn-out legal process."

"That's ridiculous," Beverly argued.

Albert didn't disagree but said, "That's the law."

The conversation lulled again, broken only when Mila said, "Thank you. Thank you for helping me. I hope your good intentions don't backfire on you."

Albert asked, "How far are we from the hotel?" Beverly had booked it months ago when they were planning their trip. She added a room for Albert when he expressed an interest in meeting them, but he had no clue where it was.

Beverly took one hand from the wheel to point ahead. "It's just around the next corner. It's a lovely place. We used to eat in the restaurant on the bottom floor all the time when we were posted here."

"They used to serve a lovely wiener schnitzel," Roy chipped in.

Albert watched Mila, observing her for any sign her story might not be true. He had no reason to disbelieve her claims, but he'd learned long ago not to accept what people report. In his experience the truth is a rare beast given freely by very few. Nevertheless, he believed her. Mila's sister was inside the old military camp where a commune of sorts had sunk their ideals deep into her brain. It didn't make them wrong, but it didn't sit well with him either.

All was quiet in the car until Mila started squawking.

"It's him! Oh, my God, it's him!" Her right arm stuck out from her body, aimed up and to the right.

Staring through the window, all Albert could see were trees. Was she hallucinating? Was she having a bad trip from some drugs she'd taken?

Beverly jolted when Mila yelled, twitching the steering wheel hard to the right and almost crashing into a parked car. Wrestling it back under control, she said, "He who?"

"Horst!" I just saw his face on a poster. "Look, there it is again!" This time when she pointed, Albert was able to follow her arm. It wasn't the trees she was aiming at, but a poster hanging from a lamppost.

Beneath the face of a middle-aged man with a politician's smile read the legend, '*Re-elect Mayor Schultz*'. He'd been captured giving the perfect politician's smile – all teeth and absolutely no warmth, like a shark trying to convince you it's vegetarian.

Albert asked, "Who is he? Other than the mayor, I mean. How do you know him, Mila?"

Mila spun around in her seat to lock eyes with Albert.

"I only know him as Horst. I couldn't have told you his last name to save my life. Everyone calls him Horst. He's the leader of Unlimited Horizons. He is intense and a little scary, but oh so charismatic. Talking to him is like having all your clothes stripped away. It always feels like he is staring right into my soul, and he truly believes he can help people if they just surrender to his way of thinking. That's what happened to my sister."

Another poster flashed by Albert's window - the same face, the same message *'Re-elect Mayor Schultz'.* The mayor of the town, which was probably nothing more than a collection of houses before the war ended and the Royal Airforce built a massive base, was also the leader of a cult.

Maybe cult was the wrong word for it, but Albert chose to label it thusly. They were arriving at their accommodation and no matter what happened next, they needed to get Mila clean and warm and wearing better clothes. She was here to get her sister, but did Talia need to be rescued?

There was no need for him to get involved. No need to do anything, really, but something about the mayor doubling as the leader of a reclusive community had his detective's brain twitching.

Chapter 4

Beverly stayed in the car with Mila while Albert and Roy checked into their rooms. Having discussed the subject with their unexpected guest, they already knew she had nowhere to stay and no clothes into which she could change. Three inches taller than Beverly and many pounds lighter, nothing the older woman had with her was going to fit, but there were shops not far from the hotel where Beverly insisted she would purchase a few essentials.

Naturally, Mila argued, but she didn't put up much of a fight. It was clear she recognised her needs and was grateful to have found people willing to help a stranger.

Inside the hotel, Albert almost enquired about an additional room. He could say his granddaughter had unexpectedly joined them. Yet he held back. If Bruno and Thomas, or indeed anyone from the camp came looking for the runaway woman, they might enquire about who was staying in the sleepy German town's hotels.

They could change things later, but for now, Roy and Albert agreed it would be better to give his room to Mila. He would sleep on the floor or the couch, or maybe the guys would bunk together leaving the girls in the other room.

The minutia could be figured out later.

Given the pick of rooms as it was off peak and the place was more than half empty, Albert selected two at the back of the building where it overlooked the carpark. Albert selected them deliberately, but if pushed to say why, he would have shied away from giving the real reason, which was that he felt ill at ease.

Yet again he was in a new place and teetering on the edge of a mystery. The only difference between this town and the last few was the addition of his friends. For once he wasn't completely alone, but rather than give him comfort, the addition of Roy and Beverly made him worry all the more.

Sensing something in his human, Rex nudged Albert's leg with his muzzle and pushed his nose into the old man's hand.

Albert scratched at the fur behind Rex's head, absentmindedly wondering what the next few days would bring.

With keys in hand, Roy and Albert returned to the carpark. They needed to get Mila inside without raising suspicion. That ought to be easy enough, but the poor woman looked homeless. There were cuts and scrapes to her arms and legs and face. Her hair was a bird's nest, and her clothes were both torn and dirty. Plus, she had nothing on her feet.

The only shoes Beverly had that would go on Mila's feet were a pair of house slippers with a lot of give. Beverly's coat hid her arms, and they used a pack of tissues and some water from Rex's travel bottle to clean up her face and legs. A hat took care of her hair. The mishmash of styles in items that didn't fit her meant she still looked homeless, but only if a person paused to take notice. They had their keys, so they passed through the small hotel's reception with barely a glance from the woman behind the counter.

Their rooms were all on the ground floor in deference to their age. It wasn't that they couldn't manage the stairs, but given the option of avoiding them altogether …

Beverly went into her room while Albert ushered Mila into his.

"I will be staying next door," he explained, holding up a hand to stop her protest before it came. "You need help, and we are happy to give it. Use the shower to get yourself clean at least. I believe Beverly is going to find a place to get you some clothes and fetch her first aid kit so you can patch your cuts. Are you hungry?"

Mila sagged. "Why are you being so kind? You don't know me. How do you even know I am telling you the truth? I could be anyone."

"I don't know if you are telling me the truth, Mila, but sometimes in life we have to take a leap of faith."

Rex nudged her hand. He wasn't even trying to work out what was going on. The subtle nuances of human behaviour were lost on him, but he understood the woman they found in the woods needed help. Humans get cold quickly and she hadn't been dressed for the conditions. Also, Mila's feet were bare, and he'd been able to smell the blood from her cuts long before he saw her. Rex remembered only too well the time he had to keep his human warm until help came. The old man spent three days in bed following that incident.

Rex understood being cold and hungry, knew what it was like to be worried. Anxiety tainted her perspiration in a way only a dog could detect. His human had accepted her into their pack, so he was here for her.

Mila had never owned a dog and couldn't claim to feel all that comfortable around them. Especially one the size of Rex. The dogs at the camp were vicious and terrifying. Too fast to outrun, Mila was amazed she'd managed to get to the fence first and didn't want to think about what might have happened if they'd caught up to her.

All the same, Albert's dog was friendly and looked at her with kind eyes.

"His name is Rex?" she sought to confirm, tentatively scratching the soft fur behind his ears.

Rex wagged his tail.

Albert looked down as his dog looked up to meet his gaze. "Yes, this is Rex. He used to be a police dog. He is very loyal and dependable. Aren't you, boy?"

Rex wagged his tail again.

"*I am indeed all those things. How about a gravy bone?*" He nudged the coat pocket where Albert kept a small stash of treats.

It made Albert grin, but he didn't argue. Producing one of the three-inch-long dog biscuits from his pocket, he offered it to be taken rather than flick it into the air for Rex to catch. It allowed him to show Mila how gentle the giant dog could be.

"Well, you should shut the door and finish warming up, Mila. I'm going to take this one for a walk." Rex probably didn't really need a walk, but they had spent hours on a train and then in Beverly's car. Their walk around the old camp's perimeter got cut short, and Albert felt it would be good for him to get some exercise even if Rex wasn't bothered.

Albert left her in the doorway to what was supposed to be his room, clicking his tongue to let Rex know they were heading out. They exited via the hotel's main door, stepping out into bright sunshine that made Albert lift an arm to shield his eyes.

He turned away from it when he reached the pavement and set off along the road. He didn't look at his watch but knew it had to be getting close to three in the afternoon. The sun was on its way down; its low position in the sky one of the reasons why it was so blinding. He would be back before it set, but doubted he would manage to lose his way around the small town even if it grew dark.

Hoffenholen the town wasn't really a town at all so far as Albert could see. It probably satisfied the definition due to population size when the RAF base was open and operating, but with the service personnel gone, there really wasn't much here. He passed a small shop, what appeared to be a pub serving food, and he could see a petrol station in the distance where it sat on the outskirts of the settlement. There were houses on both sides of the road, and streets leading off. There would be a thousand homes or maybe more than that, but not a lot more.

Rex sniffed his way through the town, sampling the air and storing what he found for later reference. He smelled the beer from the pub long before they got to it, found a squashed hedgehog in the road that was at least two days old, and was surprised to find almost no sign of any squirrels.

When they found a park, Albert sent him away to do what he needed, and let him roam for a while, using the time to compose a message to his children. Apple-Blossom, his youngest granddaughter, his daughter's 'oops' in her mid-forties, had created a group chat on something called 'WhatsApp'. Albert didn't understand any of it and the name made him think of *Bugs Bunny* every time he heard it.

Using that, he sent a message to his three children. He had to admit sending just one instead of typing it out three times was a convenient advantage.

'Hey, kids. I met with Roy and Beverly as planned and we are in Germany visiting one of the former RAF bases where Roy was stationed during the eighties. I don't want you to think I am raising a red flag, but there is something going on here. We met a woman who was running barefoot through the woods and had to climb over the old camp fence to escape two dogs and a pair of guys on bikes who were chasing her. It might be nothing, but I know how you all like to fret, so I figured why not give you

something to fret about for once. It's probably nothing, but if you get a chance, can you please look into a man called Horst Schultz. He's the mayor of Hoffenholen. And while you are at it, see if you can find out anything about a group called Unlimited Horizons. Like I said, it might be nothing …'

Albert's finger hovered over the send button. Should he alert them? He hadn't done so at his previous three stops, and he got into trouble at each of them. There was something different about Hoffenholen, though. He could sense it in the air, or in his water. Call it what you will. Call it Spideysense if it helps, Albert had a feeling in his gut that things were going to get really interesting.

He pressed send and that was when he heard it. The sound of his premonitions coming true.

Chapter 5

"Guten tag!" a voice called out, stopping Albert in his tracks. "Herr Smith, bitte!"

Across the grass, Rex looked up. Two men in uniform were approaching his human. Had it been two different men – ones not wearing clothes he could identify as those of law enforcement officers, he might have been concerned. Rex thought of the police as inherently good. They were the good guys. Or girls – Rex liked to think inclusively.

He'd just found an interesting patch of grass that smelled like seventeen different dogs had visited it in the last two days and he was building quite the olfactory map of the area. Dismissing the police officers as unimportant for now, he went back to inspecting the scent profile.

Albert turned to face the direction from which his name had been called. Two uniformed police officers were walking briskly toward him. Both were men in their thirties, fit looking individuals with the bearing of those who took their role in society seriously.

The taller of the two spoke to him. "Herr Smith? Albert Smith?"

"Yes, that's me," Albert replied, his words guarded. Should he be wary? Mila didn't want to report her dilemma to the police. Was there something more to it than she let on?

"We have been looking for you," the second officer said. His English was accented but fluent. "Would you mind coming with us, please? It will only take a short while of your time."

Engaging a polite tone, Albert asked, "May I ask what this is regarding?" So soon after discovering Mila in the woods and learning what he had about Unlimited Horizons, the timing of their request felt too convenient.

The taller officer smiled. "Just a formality. A courtesy, you might say. Your notoriety precedes you, Mr Smith, and a local dignitary wishes to meet with you."

"That wouldn't happen to be the mayor, would it?" Albert's eyes narrowed. Thus far there was no reason to believe the officers intended him any harm. Their hands were relaxed, not poised to grab their weapons as they might be if they were up to no good. But then, Albert considered, they probably didn't see him as much of a threat.

"Indeed," the taller one beamed. "You are as astute as your reputation suggests. Mayor Schultz is excited to meet such a famous detective."

Both officers turned their bodies a quarter turn, their feet angling back toward their patrol car. They expected him to acquiesce.

Albert considered his options. He had every right to simply refuse to go with them and doubted they would kick up a fuss unless he chose to be rude. That they were doing the mayor's bidding could be considered worrying, but in such a small and remote town, the mayor would have a lot of pull and their boss at the station likely had to maintain a relationship with the local politician just to get things done.

Whatever the case, Albert had a chance to talk to the man Mila believed to be behind her sister's incarceration, if that word could be employed.

"What about my dog?" Albert directed their attention to Rex who looked up to see the three humans looking his way.

"Your dog is welcome to join us," the taller officer answered with a tight smile. "It is no problem."

Rex wandered over to the police officers, his ears twitching as he tried to figure out what was going on. His training as a police dog made him naturally inclined to trust anyone in uniform, but there was a tension in Albert's posture that made him wary.

"Very well," Albert agreed. "Lead the way."

The officers indicated their patrol car. It was parked directly in front of the pub, its paintwork gleaming in the late afternoon sunlight. Opening the rear door, one officer gestured for Albert to climb in. Rex followed, settling on the seat next to his human with a quiet huff. Albert stroked his fur, thankful to have Rex at his side.

The car moved off, heading not back toward the town centre as Albert expected, but in the opposite direction. The houses thinned as they left Hoffenholen behind, and within three minutes they were approaching a high fence Albert recognised instantly. It was the same one over which Mila escaped an hour ago.

"I see," Albert murmured, more to himself than to anyone else.

The officers drove to a gate that opened as they approached. Beyond it was a well-maintained driveway leading to what had once been the administrative buildings of RAF Hoffenholen. The woodland through which Mila was chased surrounded it on all sides but the front.

Albert took note of the security guards minding the gate. They had sidearms. Looking around he saw cameras positioned at intervals along the road. There were more than he expected for a spiritual retreat. Remembering the barbed wire fence, Albert noted the former military base had retained many of its security features, some of which had been updated with modern technology. He questioned why they would be necessary?

The car pulled up outside a large, imposing building. Two storeys high, it was a squat, functional structure that undoubtedly started its life as part of the military infrastructure. However, the windows now bore colourful curtains and there were raised beds with flowers along the front façade.

The flowers were sparse at this time of the year, but Albert could imagine the beds in full bloom come spring and summer.

"If you would follow us, please," the taller officer said as they exited the car. "Your dog is welcome inside."

Albert moved his head close to Rex's ear and whispered, "Stay close."

Rex looked up, meeting the old man's gaze and holding it for a moment. There was something about their situation he was misreading. Were they in danger? He sniffed the air, looking for anything that might indicate trouble. But the tell-tale whiff of human fear was absent.

Exiting the car, Albert kept Rex's lead short. Inside his head, he assured himself they were in no danger. It wasn't as if they would attempt to make him disappear.

Would they?

His heart rate spiking, despite his instruction for it to stay calm, Albert followed the policemen into the building. The interior was surprisingly plush, with expensive carpeting underfoot and tasteful artwork on the walls. It was a far cry from the utilitarian military facility it had once been.

Inside the building, Albert could hear a voice. It echoed in the corridor. He couldn't make out the words, but there was something captivating about it. *Entrancing* was another word that sprang to mind.

The police officers crossed the foyer and started up the stairs, ascending them to access the second floor. Paying no attention to what Albert was doing – they obviously expected that he would follow – Albert turned left toward the voice.

The voice grew louder and clearer and he began to make out words. A man with a voice like waxed silk spoke of letting go of the problems of the past, of embracing the opportunity to be renewed, and facing down the demons that beset each and every one of us.

His pace hurried for he knew the officers would notice his absence and double back, Albert found the source of the voice just as they found him.

"Hey!" one called, but Albert ignored his cry, ducking through an open doorway to arrive at the back of a room full of people.

The room was carpeted in what could only be described as the most depressing shade of brown ever conceived, as if someone had specifically requested 'the colour of disappointment' from a particularly unimaginative carpet salesman. The walls were painted white, continuing the theme of death by boredom, but in contrast, the man speaking exuded energy and excitement from every pore.

There were perhaps thirty people facing a man who stood on a platform. He was on his feet addressing a crowd who listened intently to his every word. They sat on plastic chairs arranged in rows that curved slightly toward the edges to wrap around the stage. He looked over and smiled when Albert came in.

There was no mistaking who the man was. Albert had seen his picture on a re-election poster less than an hour ago. Mayor Horst Schultz was in his mid-fifties, with salt-and-pepper hair and the confident bearing of someone accustomed to authority. He wore an expensive suit that Albert could see had been tailored to his frame.

He returned his attention to the room. "Brothers and sisters, I encourage you all to let go of your pain. Here you have the opportunity to free yourself from the shackles that have bound you, to cast off your old life and embrace a new one that will give you a level of fulfilment you cannot yet perceive. You all came here of your own accord because you need to find a new purpose and we can give that to you through the medium of digital ascension."

The police officers eased their way into the room behind Albert and Rex, taking up position either side of them. Albert thought they were about to demand he follow them again when Horst turned his attention their way. He gave an almost imperceptible shake of his head, and the police officers took a step back.

It confirmed Albert's concern that the mayor might have control over the local police and made him question whether they were also part of the movement.

Meeting the eyes of the seated attendees, Horst asked, "Are you ready to believe?"

The reply came as one voice as though it had been rehearsed, "We are ready." They sounded brainwashed and a chill crept up Albert's spine.

Lifting his eyes, the mayor looked directly at Albert.

"Good day, Sir. Thank you for joining us. I will meet with you shortly. Unless you wish to join us?" He lifted his left hand to beckon Albert forward.

Albert held his ground.

"All are welcome here, Mr Smith. All can benefit from embracing our way of life, our digital ascension."

Dozens of responses zipped through Albert's mind. He had no experience of such things from which he could base an opinion, but he had one all the same: this was a cult. Precisely what Mila said, and it was worse than he thought.

Taking a step back, Albert said, "I think our meeting would be better in private."

Chapter 6

Once again following the police officers, though this time they kept a close eye to make sure he didn't wander off, they climbed a set of stairs to reach the upper floor and walked down a wide corridor, passing several closed doors, before stopping outside one that bore a brass plaque reading 'Facilitator's Office' in both German and English. The tall officer knocked and opened the door without waiting for a response. He stepped back, welcoming Albert and Rex to step inside. Both men followed him in, taking positions close to the door where they stood in silence like a pair of sentinels.

Or guards.

A woman with a tablet in her hand came forward. Unlike the police officers she wasn't smiling and gave off the air of someone who had far too much to do to be wasting time dealing with Albert. Blonde hair fell in salon styled locks to six inches below her shoulders. She had the figure of a swimwear model and a face that could grace a billboard advertising makeup. She wore a grey pencil skirt above stockings and four-inch heels and a long-sleeved silk shirt in a bright sky blue. Pinned high on her shirt to the right of the second button was a small square plastic device. Albert could see the electronics within it.

"Mr Smith, I'm Sabrina Aldridge. I'm Horst's personal assistant and executive manager". She didn't extend her hand to be shaken. "This will have to be a quick appointment, Mr Smith."

"It can be no appointment at all if you prefer," Albert replied, his tone even. "I didn't ask to be brought here."

If Sabrina had any thoughts on the matter, she kept them to herself. "Horst will be along momentarily." Her accent wasn't German, and her English was impeccable.

Her looks were Scandinavian, but Albert didn't trust himself to state that was her heritage.

Left to kill time, Albert used it to look around. The office was large and luxuriously appointed. Floor-to-ceiling windows looked out over the grounds, and bookshelves lined one wall from floor to ceiling. A massive desk dominated one end of the room. Behind the desk was a large oil painting of the mayor. No, Albert realised, it wasn't the mayor at all, but one of his ancestors.

The figure in the oil painting had the same face, but with a few minor changes. The nose was broader, the eyebrows closer set. Captured standing next to an ornately embroidered chair, a sword hung from his belt. The man was dressed in military uniform from a different age when bright colours for visibility, rather than muted ones for the opposite effect, were the fashion. Gold brocade adorned his epaulettes and sleeves.

Rex sniffed the air. He could smell cigar smoke and traces of ash where some had fallen to the carpet. In the bin was an apple core, most likely from today though it was possible it was left over from the previous evening. He could smell Sabrina's perfume and the mix of sweat and deodorant coming from the two police officers.

There was another smell, he detected. That of a cat. Except it wasn't a cat. It was cat like, but somehow also something more. He needed to give it more thought but was interrupted by the door opening.

Mayor Horst Schultz entered the room looking just as passive, serene, and completely in control as he had downstairs.

"Ah!" he looked overjoyed to see Albert and came at him with both hands extended. "The great Albert Smith!"

Albert accepted the handshake but said very little. He didn't … couldn't think of himself as the great anything. Sure, he'd solved a mystery that got him into the papers and gave away a stack of money that he didn't need and should never have been his. That didn't make him great. Just aware of the world and how it ought to work.

Albert shook the offered hand, noting the firm, confident grip. "A pleasure," he replied, though he wasn't sure if he believed it was true.

"I am delighted to meet you, Albert. May I call you Albert?" he enquired, not waiting for Albert to respond. "Of course you already know who I am but let me introduce myself formally. I'm Horst Schultz, mayor of Hoffenholen and facilitator of Unlimited Horizons. Please, do take a seat." He walked to his desk, rounding it to sit in the large wooden chair on the other side. Like Sabrina and the police officers, his English was near perfect, though his words came with a distinctly German accent.

As Albert sat in one of the comfortable leather chairs facing the desk, Rex's nose twitched. He couldn't let the feline scent go. He'd been willing to dismiss it, but the new man now talking to his human – a man who was clearly the alpha – stank of it. He shot a glance toward a partially open door at the far side of the office, his hackles rising slightly.

"I see your dog has detected my pet," Schultz said with amusement. "He is most perceptive."

"Your pet?" Albert enquired, following Rex's gaze to the door.

"A somewhat unconventional companion," Schultz admitted. "But we all have our eccentricities, do we not? My great grandfather," Horst used his right arm to indicate the oil painting behind his head, "was a baron who served in the court of Keizer Wilhelm the second. You see, I come from a long line of gentlemen, Albert, and I recognise in you much of what I see in myself. It is for that reason that I asked you here today. I hope that we can act as gentlemen."

His eyes narrowing slightly as he tried to guess where the mayor was trying to take their conversation, Albert said, "I'm sure we can."

"Excellent! Now, Mr. Smith, I understand you had an … encounter with one of our community residents today."

Albert considered his response carefully. "If you're referring to the young woman being chased through the woods by motorcycles and dogs, then yes, I did."

Schultz laughed; a warm, charming sound that failed to reach his eyes. "I can imagine how it might have appeared to an outsider. Mila is … troubled, for want of a better word. She joined our community seeking help, but the path to enlightenment is not always easy, and sometimes our residents experience moments of doubt or confusion."

"She seemed rather determined to leave."

"Yes, well," Schultz sighed dramatically. "Mila has a history of impulsive behaviour. Her sister has been with us for some time now and has made remarkable progress. We had hoped Mila would find similar peace here. I understand you're concerned, Mr. Smith," the mayor continued. "It does you credit. But I assure you, Unlimited Horizons is a registered spiritual community. We help people who have lost their way. With us they find meaning and purpose. Sometimes that process involves breaking old patterns of behaviour, and that can be challenging."

"And the dogs and motorcycles chasing Mila?" Albert pressed.

"Security personnel," Schultz explained smoothly. "For her own safety. The woods can be dangerous, and in her confused state, she might have harmed herself. We were simply trying to bring her back to where she could be properly cared for. Now, regarding Mila. I would very much like to speak with her. For her own well-being, you understand. Her sister is quite concerned."

"Is she? Perhaps I could speak with her. I have a message to pass on from Mila."

"I can deliver it."

"No, I think it would be best if I speak with her myself. Mila was quite concerned about her sister's health and wellbeing."

"Those are not things you or Mila need to worry about, Talia has never been in better health."

"Then let me see her," Albert pressed. He was convinced the mayor would deny him but wanted to see how far he could push it. Was it possible to find a crack in his armour?

From behind Albert, Sabrina said, "I'm afraid that won't be possible, Mr Smith. Talia is still ascending. That is why Mila was prevented from interacting with her. A disturbance at this time could set Talia back weeks. Mila refused to listen to our pleas. Her sister needs to be here and is getting better every day. Did you know she was a drug addict when she arrived here? That she had an alcohol dependency? Talia is clean for the first time in almost a decade, and she is happy."

Unlike her boss, Sabrina delivered her words with hard eyes and a challenging tone.

Albert's eyes never left the mayor's and when Sabrina stopped speaking Horst repeated his request.

"I need to speak with Mila, Albert. Please tell me where she is so we can bring her back to safety."

"I'm afraid I can't help you there," Albert replied calmly. "After your security personnel chased her through the woods, she seemed quite determined to get away. We parted company shortly thereafter."

Schultz's smile didn't waiver, but his eyes visibly hardened. "I see. Well, if you do happen to encounter her again, please do encourage her to return to us. Her journey here was only just beginning, and there is so much more she could gain from our community."

"I'll bear that in mind."

"Excellent." Schultz rose from his chair. "Well, I won't keep you any longer, Mr. Smith. I simply wanted to introduce myself and clear up any misunderstandings about what you witnessed today. Hoffenholen is a peaceful town, and Unlimited Horizons is a vital part of our community. I hope you enjoy the remainder of your stay."

Albert remained in his chair.

"What is digital ascension?"

The mayor's face froze and a muscle in his jaw twitched, but the show of negative emotion lasted for only the briefest of moments before the calm exterior returned. Albert thought he would return to his chair, but Horst Schultz chose instead to walk around the desk. He came to stand in front of Albert where he sat back on the edge of the desk, very much in Albert's personal space.

It was a move designed to intimidate. Albert ignored it.

When his guest showed no sign of discomfort, the mayor started to talk.

"Digital ascension, Albert, is the process of surrendering one's worldly identity and contributing to a new digital consciousness that leads to spiritual enlightenment. Downstairs, our newest members are embracing that very concept, casting off their debt, their bills, the earthly ties that shackle them. They will be untied from the pressures life has brought them and be able to move forward unencumbered. Unlimited Horizons and the practices we teach are a joy to behold, Albert. If you wish, I can show you a world where nothing and no one will ever bother you again."

Albert stood, maintaining a calm exterior despite the alarm bells ringing in his head. The mayor's smooth explanation sounded plausible, but it contrasted sharply with Mila's terror and desperate flight, and he didn't believe a word of it.

"Thank you for your time, Mayor Schultz," Albert said, offering his hand again. "It's been … illuminating."

"The pleasure was mine," Schultz replied, shaking Albert's hand firmly. "Oh, and Mr. Smith? Do enjoy your visit with your friends, the Hopes. It's been some time since Roy was last in Hoffenholen, I believe."

Albert's face betrayed nothing, but internally he registered the implied message. Schultz knew exactly who he was and who he was with. It wasn't a threat—not explicitly—but it was certainly meant to let Albert know that very little escaped the mayor's notice. It was another attempt to intimidate him, and it was working.

"I'll be sure to give them your regards." Albert kept the mayor's gaze for a few seconds, wondering what he might see behind his eyes. He was a politician, so Albert expected a certain slipperiness, but Horst was far more than that. He was a cult leader and was about as scary as any person Albert had ever met.

Releasing the mayor's hand, Albert turned to find Sabrina watching him with what he could only describe as barely contained contempt. She looked like she wanted to squish him, much like a bug.

The pair of police officers took their cue, opening the door and waiting for Albert to exit so they could escort him back to their car.

Driving back through the gates of Unlimited Horizons, Albert gazed out at the fence surrounding the compound, wondering just what secrets lay within and how deeply Mila's sister was entangled in them.

Rex pressed against his leg, sensing his human's disquiet. Albert absentmindedly scratched behind his ears, his mind already turning over what he had learned and what his next steps should be. One thing was certain—Mayor Horst Schultz was not simply the benevolent spiritual leader he portrayed himself to be, and

Unlimited Horizons was far more than a simple retreat for troubled souls. The question was, what was really happening behind those fences, and how was he going to find out?

Chapter 7

Mayor Horst Schultz watched the patrol car leave his compound and turn right. He watched it through the trees that bordered the road until it was out of sight.

Next to him, Sabrina asked, "Do you think he knows anything?"

Horst cocked an eyebrow. "How can he? Mila didn't know anything."

"Then why is he here? In Hoffenholen, I mean?"

"He is meeting with his friends, the Hopes. I genuinely believe there is nothing more to it than that. Albert Smith's presence is purely a coincidence."

Sabrina pursed her lips and skewed them to one side, deep in thought.

"You seem worried, my dear. Would you like to book a private therapy session with me?"

She rolled her eyes and started to walk away. "I'm not one of the brainless idiots that falls for your inane nonsense, Horst. I know what digital ascension really is." She paused halfway to the door. "You need to take his involvement seriously. You know what he has done and what he is capable of. If he was lying about Mila, which he probably was, he may plan to continue poking his nose in."

Horst turned his attention back to the view outside. It was a pleasant enough day and the clouds were lifting, threatening to reveal the sun.

"Oh, I don't think you should worry too much about Albert Smith."

"And why is that, Horst?"

"Because he's a professional busybody, Sabrina. He doesn't have the backing of the police. He has no authority to poke his nose in … it's a dangerous habit to have. Who knows what might happen to him."

"Let me guess. Another duel?"

Horst glanced behind his desk to the thin fencer's epee hanging on a hook in the corner. A sly smile pulled the left side of his mouth into a devilish smile.

"Perhaps."

Chapter 8

"I'm not going back there," Mila crossed her arms over her chest, her eyes narrowing at the very suggestion. "You can't make me."

The hotel room Albert gave up for her felt like sanctuary, and she was prepared to defend it. Her hair no longer looked like a bird's nest and still bore faint traces of dampness from the shower. She wore a pair of sweatpants and a t-shirt Beverly purchased for her. They were loose, suggesting Beverly had made her best guess at Mila's size and got it wrong, but they were clean at least.

"I'm not suggesting you return to the compound," Albert replied in a calm voice. "But I need you to tell us everything you know about Unlimited Horizons. Any detail could be helpful, no matter how small."

Albert, Roy, and Beverly were gathered in Albert's hotel room – though technically it was now Mila's – to debrief after Albert's unexpected meeting with the mayor. Albert sat in the chair by the window while Roy and Beverly perched on the edge of the bed. Rex had stretched out on the carpet, though his eyes remained alert, watching the humans with interest.

"What did the mayor say about Talia?" Mila asked, her voice tight with worry.

Albert repeated the conversation as accurately as he could. "He said she was still ascending and that disturbing her now would be detrimental to her recovery."

Roy screwed up his face. "Sounds like a load of new-age hippie nonsense to me."

Mila, however, nodded. "That's what they told me every time I enquired about seeing her."

"But you never got to see her?" Beverly sought to clarify, her face creased with question.

"No," Mila's voice cracked slightly, the emotional strain showing. "They kept saying she was in a different section and that I wasn't ready to join her yet. I was there for two months and never got to find her. They keep the newbies separate."

"Why?" asked Beverly.

Mila huffed out a hard and frustrated breath. "Some nonsense about ascension again. We had to qualify to proceed to join the community. I was in one section and Talia was in another. Everyone else I came in with left me behind. I think they knew I didn't believe any of the things they were saying."

Albert stroked his chin thoughtfully. "Sabrina mentioned Talia had drug and alcohol problems. Is that true?"

Mila's shoulders slumped. "Yes. She's been struggling for years. We're from Belarus originally. Our parents died when we were teenagers, and Talia didn't cope well. I've been trying to help her, but it's been difficult."

"So how did she end up here?" Roy asked, leaning forward with his elbows on his knees.

"She met someone online who told her about this place. Said it could help her get clean. When I didn't hear from her for weeks, I got worried and tracked her across Europe. I found the compound and they let me in after I told them who I was, but then…" She shuddered. "They kept me isolated, took my things, and started making me attend sessions where they talked about the whole digital ascension thing."

Rex perked up his ears. He noticed the change in the woman's scent – the sour tang of fear mixing with her natural odour. Something about the memory disturbed her. He rose and padded over to place his head on her knee, offering canine comfort in the way he knew best.

Mila seemed surprised by the gesture but tentatively placed her hand on Rex's head. "Thanks, Rex."

Albert watched the interaction with a small smile before returning to business. "Did you see anything unusual while you were there? Anything that might indicate they're doing anything other than what they say?"

Mila furrowed her brow in concentration. "Not really. I was shut off from the main compound as I just said, but there were gaps in the fence, and I kept looking through them hoping to spot Talia. When they weren't looking, that is." Mila stopped talking, her face thoughtful for a few moments before she said, "There are rooms under the ground."

"Underground?" asked Albert.

Before she could answer, Roy said, "Yes. In fact, there's a whole rabbit warren of them." Seeing the faces around him, including his wife's who made it clear she had no clue what he was talking about, Roy did his best to explain. "Remember this is a military installation built during the Cold War. There are bunkers below ground designed specifically to withstand a nuclear strike. I only saw a part of it during my time at the base, but it's extensive. It's like a small town down there."

Albert sucked some air between his teeth. "So they could be up to anything, and no one would ever know. Not even satellites passing overhead would be able to see their operation." Albert couldn't provide a tangible reason why he suspected there might be something more going on, but it felt right to be suspicious. Unlimited Horizons was helping people and Horst made it sound entirely altruistic. Albert judged the man to have hidden motives, not least because anyone that charismatic and narcissistic had to be up to something. Also, why was Sabrina so hostile? Plus, they had the new initiates surrender their identification. It felt … wrong.

Roy just shrugged.

Beverly, still frowning, asked, "How come you've never mentioned these bunkers before?"

Roy offered her an apologetic expression. "Official Secrets Act, my love. I probably shouldn't be telling you now."

"Well, I'm glad you did," said Albert, turning the conversation back to Mila. "Did you hear anything? Snippets of conversation that might not have meant anything at the time, but in the context of what we have just learned …"

Mila opened her mouth and closed it again, her eyes looking at nothing in the room, but focused on the past.

"I'm not sure if it's relevant, but I did hear one conversation. It stuck with me because Sabrina heard them and got angry. She told them to shut up and never speak again, like they had just spilled some big secret."

Keen to tease the information from her, Albert asked, "What were they talking about, Mila?"

"I'm not sure, but I remember one of them used the term processing packages and another said something about extraction rates."

"Drugs?" Roy suggested.

"I don't think so," Mila shook her head. "The way they were talking made it seem more like data. Information."

Albert exchanged glances with Roy and Beverly. "What exactly did you see in terms of computer equipment?"

"Nothing. Beyond a few tablets people like Sabrina carried and an occasional laptop, I saw almost no technology at all. I think they had to eschew it because they preached the concept of throwing off our digital presence." Her face went distant again, her expression that of a person dredging their memory. "They wear little badges."

"Badges?" Roy questioned.

Mila looked up. "Yeah, but not like a political party pin. I mean like the kind that access doors you can't get through without the right clearance. Sabrina wore one ..."

"I saw it today," Albert remarked. "I didn't see one on Horst, but Mila is right. They are the kind of badge that contains a code to get you through an electronic barrier."

The conversation fell into a lull, no one saying anything for more than a minute.

Beverly broke the silence when she reached out to pat Mila's hand. "You've been very brave, dear. And you've given us some useful information."

Albert stood up and moved to the window, peering out at the darkening sky. "I think we need to learn more about our friend Mayor Schultz and his assistant Sabrina Aldridge."

"*I'm hungry,*" announced Rex, nudging Albert's hand with his nose. The humans had been talking for quite some time, and while the conversation was obviously important, a dog had needs.

Albert glanced down at his furry companion and smiled. "I think a dinner break is in order. We could all use something to eat while we consider our next steps."

"I know a place," Roy said, rising to his feet. "German food, but you won't be disappointed, Albert. They do a schnitzel the size of a dinner plate."

"Sounds perfect," Albert replied, though his mind was still churning with thoughts of what might be happening at Unlimited Horizons.

"What about me?" asked Mila. "Is it safe for me to go out?"

"I can stay with her," volunteered Beverly. "I have a pack of cards," she reported brightly. "We can play a few hands of cribbage."

Looking confused, Mila said, "I don't know how to play that."

Beverly wasn't even slightly put off. "That's not a problem. As long as you can count, it's easy. I'll teach you."

"We'll hit the takeaway instead," said Roy, donning his coat. "What shall I bring you?"

"You should stop for a meal," Beverly insisted. "Albert came all this way ..."

"That hardly matters," Albert countered, "but it's not a bad idea for us to eat out. I want to see if they are watching us." He didn't need to explain who 'they' were.

"Okay," Roy surrendered. "We'll be quick though. I'm sure Mila must be hungry, my love, even if you're not."

Voice timid, Mila asked, "Do you really think they're looking for me?"

"I'd be surprised if they weren't," Albert replied honestly. "You'll be safe here for now, but keep the door locked and don't answer it unless it's one of us. I don't think the mayor knows where you are, but I wouldn't put it past him to have people looking."

Food was discussed and meals decided. As the men filed from the room, Albert gave Rex his bowl of doggy chow and told him to stay. He would walk him when he returned but wanted the dog to remain behind as added protection for the ladies.

Rex heard what his human said but was too busy burrowing through his meal to see that he'd been left behind.

Chapter 9

Albert's schnitzel was as large as Roy promised, hanging over the edge of the plate like a map of a small European country. Beside it was a small mountain of German potato salad, and a side dish of sauerkraut.

"It's impressive," Albert admitted, wondering if he could possibly finish it.

"Best in town," Roy said with evident satisfaction. "I used to be on first-name terms with the owner, though I haven't seen him yet. I suppose he might have retired."

The restaurant was cozy and dimly lit, with wooden beams crossing the ceiling and an impressive array of beer steins displayed along one wall. It was exactly what Albert expected a German Gasthaus to look like, right down to the rosy-cheeked waitresses in traditional dress.

They had just tucked into their food when Albert's phone began to vibrate in his pocket. Fishing it out, he checked the display.

"It's my son," he said, showing the screen to Roy. "Would you excuse me for a moment?"

Roy nodded, his mouth already full of schnitzel.

Albert stepped outside into the cool evening air. "Hello, Gary."

"Dad," his son's voice betrayed his relief. "You're not dead or in jail then."

"Not so far, but the day isn't done yet," Albert fired back a flippant response.

"You can't blame me for worrying, Dad. You've only been in Germany for one day and you're already mixed up in something suspicious."

Albert could hear the mixture of exasperation and concern in his son's voice.

"It's nothing I can't handle, son."

"Is that supposed to make me feel better?" Gary sighed. "Look, I did some digging into this Mayor Schultz and his organization for you."

Albert's interest piqued. "And?"

"And there's nothing, Dad. Absolutely nothing suspicious on paper. Unlimited Horizons is registered as a spiritual wellness retreat. They file tax returns, have all the proper permits, and pay their bills on time. The mayor himself is a respected community leader with no criminal record. He's been re-elected three times."

"That can't be right," Albert murmured. "What about reports of missing persons?"

"None associated with the retreat," Gary replied. "I checked international databases too, since you mentioned the young woman and her sister are from Belarus. Nothing has been reported."

"What about this digital ascension business?"

"It appears to be their spiritual philosophy. According to their website, it's about 'freeing oneself from digital dependency and finding true connection in a simpler life'. There's nothing suspicious about that either."

Albert's brow furrowed. "It doesn't make sense. Mila was terrified when we met her. They were chasing her with motorcycles and attack dogs."

"I'm not saying you're wrong, Dad," Gary's voice softened. "Just that whatever's going on there, they're keeping it well hidden. They present a perfect public face."

"The best criminals usually do."

"Just be careful, will you? And keep me updated. I've got some feelers out with Interpol, but without something concrete, there's not much I can do from here."

"I appreciate your help, son."

After ending the call, Albert returned to the table, his expression thoughtful.

"Everything all right?" Roy asked, pouring Albert another glass of German beer from the pitcher they were sharing.

Albert explained what Gary had told him. "It seems Mayor Schultz has created a perfect façade."

Roy nodded. "Not surprising. The Germans are efficient, and criminals doubly so. If there is something illegal happening at that compound, they've gone to great lengths to hide it."

They ate in silence for a few minutes, both men lost in thought.

"I've been thinking about what Mila said," Albert reported. "About processing packages and extraction rates. She said she didn't think it was drugs and suggested it could be data. Like digital data, I assume."

Roy paused, his fork halfway to his mouth. "You mean like data theft?"

"It kind of fits with this digital ascension nonsense. But what would they do with it?" The answer, he knew, was one any of his kids would be able to supply. He'd retired long enough ago that digital crimes and terms like forensic accountancy were yet to be dreamed up.

Roy put down his knife and fork and picked up his drink, holding it with both hands but not drinking. He waited for Albert to look up.

"You know, old boy, Mila could just be wrong. She admitted her sister has a history of drug and alcohol abuse and you said they claimed Talia is now clean."

"That's what they said."

Roy put his drink down. "I saw that poor girl running through the wood, Albert. We all did, but what if there is nothing to this? What if there is no big crime being hidden under the guise of a cultish community? How far do we take this? I'm all for helping those in need, but I lived here for years and apart from the military withdrawing, it seems no different. It's hard to believe there is something sinister going on despite what Mila claims to have overheard."

Albert didn't respond straight away. He'd met the mayor, the same man who operated as the facilitator of the community, and there was something very off about him. He wasn't overtly threatening, but …

Before Albert could articulate his thoughts into words, Roy's phone started ringing. It was from Beverly.

"Everything all right, my love?"

"Someone's watching the hotel!" Beverly hissed loud enough that Albert heard what she said from across the table. "There's a man in a car across the street. He's been there for twenty minutes."

Chapter 10

Cautiously, Roy asked, "How do you know he's watching the hotel, my love? Are you sure it's not a taxi waiting to pick someone up?"

Roy held his head away from the phone when Beverly's terse reply blasted into his ear.

"That's a no then?" Roy pushed his luck.

Growling softly, Beverly said, "Wing Commander Hope, get back here now or so help me I will smother you in your sleep. And you'd better have something for us to eat because I'm half-starved from lack of food." The line went dead.

"We should get back," said Roy, signalling for the waitress to bring their bill.

Albert listened to his friend muttering under his breath. Roy was absolutely right that his wife instructed them to stop and have a meal. Her delayed dinner was a problem of her own making, but Albert knew he would give anything to have his dear Petunia back to grumble at him for doing precisely as she'd asked. She was never perfect, and neither was he, but their marriage had been a happy one and life wasn't the same without her.

They collected meals for the ladies from the fast-food counter at the side of the restaurant, but leaving the building, Albert noticed a black Mercedes G-Wagon parked down the street. Its windows were tinted a dark black to make seeing inside impossible.

"Roy," he murmured, nodding toward the car. "I think the ladies aren't the only ones being watched."

Roy glanced casually in the direction Albert indicated. "I see it."

They walked at a normal pace, but Albert could feel eyes on them. The car remained where it was, not moving, but Albert had no doubt it was there because of them. They turned right at the next corner and the sound of an engine starting confirmed Albert's suspicions.

"They're following us," he said.

"Let's split up," Roy suggested. "You go left at the next junction, I'll go right. See which one of us they follow."

Albert nodded, and when they reached the next crossroads, they went their separate ways. Albert walked briskly, resisting the urge to look over his shoulder. After a hundred yards, he finally heard the car. It was moving slowly down the street Roy had taken.

Doubling back, Albert arrived at the hotel twenty minutes later to find Roy already waiting in the lobby.

"Lost them in the park," Roy reported with a hint of satisfaction.

"Did you see who it was?"

"Couldn't see through the tinted windows," Roy admitted. "But someone is keeping tabs on us."

In the hotel room they found Beverly and Mila, but they weren't playing cards. They were shoulder to shoulder at the small table, crowded in next to each other to stare at Beverly's laptop.

Rex bounded over to Albert, delighted to see him. "*I kept them safe,*" he reported. "*Not that I had to do anything.*"

Beverly crossed the room to wrap her husband in a hug. Albert placed the food on the table next to Mila.

"You should eat," he said.

Mila wasted no time, digging into the bag to find a schnitzel and pommes. The sauerkraut was in a separate pot to stop it from making the rest of the food soggy.

"This is great. Thanks," she mumbled around a handful of the crispy potato fries.

"The car left ten minutes ago," said Beverly. "Almost directly after I told you about it in fact."

Roy went to the curtains, pulling them back to look outside. Albert joined him.

"There's no one out there now, old boy."

Albert put a hand on Roy's shoulder. "But they know where we are."

Mila looked frightened. "They know I'm here, don't they?"

"Not necessarily," Albert reassured her. "They might just be keeping an eye on us because we're asking questions."

"On that subject," said Beverly, taking her own meal from the bag and settling back at the laptop, "we did some digging."

Albert felt his eyebrows rise, wondering what the ladies would have to report.

"We didn't find anything," mumbled Mila around a mouthful of food.

Albert said, "Okay," and wondered if there was a big 'however' coming.

"However," said Beverly. "We then tried to find Sabrina Aldridge and her profile looks fake."

"Fake how?" Albert had no idea how to spot a fake online profile.

"Well," Mila cleared her mouth and had a sip from a glass of red wine. Albert hadn't noticed the ladies were drinking until that point, but knew Beverly was partial to a drop. "Her profile looks real when you first see it." She turned the laptop so Albert could see.

There were pictures of the blonde woman he met earlier that day. He was familiar with the platform, though he wasn't on it himself and doubted he ever would be. There were posts about her life, tagged locations to show where she had been, and a few other snippets of information.

"Her profile is public," Mila explained, "which is surprising given how they preach digital ascension. It's even up to date. The most recent post is less than a week old."

"So what makes you think it's fake?" Albert still had no clue.

Mila clicked on a different tab at the top of the screen, taking them to a new platform.

"Because on this profile, everything is exactly the same." Mila pointed. "Same pictures in the same order. Same small selection of pictures from when she was younger. Same basic information. It's all exactly the same, like they were written once and copied across. And this is just what I picked out from an initial search. Give me some time and I could probably prove it."

"Why would someone fake their online profile?" asked Roy, sounding equally bewildered.

Albert chewed his lip. He had no idea.

Rex nudged his way between the humans. "*If no one is planning to eat that ...*"

Seeing his dog eyeing the uneaten food hungrily, Albert said, "You already had dinner, dog. Nothing now until bedtime biscuits. You know the rules."

Rex frowned.

"It's for your own good, buddy." Albert ruffled the fur on the top of Rex's head. "I think, though, that it's time you got some exercise."

Rex's ears pricked up. "*Super. A walk sounds great. Let's go.*" He trotted to the door, his tail wagging.

"In a little while though, Rex. We need to plan first."

"Plan?" Roy cocked an eyebrow.

Albert nodded thoughtfully. "I believe I would like to get a closer look at the Unlimited Horizons compound."

Chapter 11

In the world of amateur detective work, nothing quite says 'brilliant idea' like two over-the-hill old men and a dog breaking into the compound of a suspicious and possibly criminal cult in the dead of night. But that's precisely what Albert, Roy, and Rex were about to do.

It was cold out. The kind of cold that makes one's bits retreat so far north they practically wave hello to the tonsils. But there they were, Albert, Roy and Rex, crouched by a fence that had been designed by someone who really, really didn't want visitors.

Inspecting the fence, Albert mused that the person responsible for it could easily also be the buffoon responsible for child-proof medicine bottles. Not for the first time since setting out, he questioned his sanity.

He believed wholeheartedly that there was something distinctly clandestine and probably criminal about the Unlimited Horizons' operation, but once they cut the fence it was going to be very hard to claim it was an accidental break in. 'Oops, Mr Police Officer, I appear to have tripped and sliced through the steel mesh with my razor-sharp wit,' wasn't going to cut it.

Unfortunately, having suggested the idea to Roy, the former RAF Wing Commander was utterly determined to see the task through. It wasn't the first time Albert had witnessed Roy's youthful roguishness return.

"This way," Roy whispered, moving with the stealth of a man who clearly hadn't received the memo about being seventy-something. Albert followed behind, making approximately the same amount of noise as a heavily sedated church mouse.

Rex, meanwhile, was in his element. If dogs could apply for jobs at MI6, he'd be the one wearing the tiny tuxedo and ordering martinis at the staff Christmas party.

His ears swivelled like miniature radar dishes, picking up sounds that humans couldn't possibly detect – including the faint whimper of Albert's knees as they protested his late-night adventure.

Nocturnal creatures scampered here and there, freezing all motion when they detected the near-silent humans moving through the darkened woodland.

Tripping on an unseen root, Albert pitched forward, voicing an unintentionally loud expletive when he hit the ground.

"Everything all right back there, old boy?" Roy enquired with a whisper.

"Marvellous," muttered Albert, picking himself up and looking for something upon which to wipe whatever now coated the palm of his right hand.

The fence loomed before them like the final boss in a particularly frustrating video game. Roy produced a pair of wire cutters from his pocket with a flourish. They were purchased at the petrol station when they set off from the hotel. Beverly filled their tank and bought the tool along with two torches, a chocolate bar, and another bottle of wine which she insisted she needed for her nerves. She was very much against the late-night excursion and predicted it would end in Roy and Albert's mutual incarceration. Or worse.

"You said the guards were armed, Albert!" she had pointed out more than once.

The wire cutters made a noise that, to Albert's terror-heightened senses, was like a heavy metal drummer warming up, though he knew in reality the sound they made was barely audible.

Rex slipped through the fence opening with the grace of a furry Olympic gymnast. Albert followed with considerably less elegance, making a mental note to add 'fence-climbing' to the list of skills that had deteriorated with age. It sat alongside 'getting up from low chairs' and 'remembering why he walked into a room'.

The compound stretched before them like an abandoned film set for a particularly depressing post-apocalyptic thriller. They crept through the woodland, keeping their pace slow and listening for any patrols prowling the grounds.

Rex ambled back and forth, trotting ahead and doubling back to make sure the slow humans were following.

"Come on, old people, this is exciting!"

Albert gave his dog a pat and reminded him of the need to stay quiet. "We're not supposed to be here, Rex," he explained. "Getting caught won't do us any good."

Darting away again, Rex marked a tree. Finding his way back would be easy without the scent trail, but he left it anyway.

Five minutes ticked by and through the trees they began to make out the dim glow of lights. A minute later they reached the edge of the trees and stopped. Most buildings were dark inside, but overhead lights – another leftover from the days when it was a military base – illuminated the exteriors and the surrounding streets so anything moving would be visible.

"That's where they took me," Albert pointed to the squat building facing the front gates. "That's where the mayor's office is. I think we need to go there."

"That's the base headquarters," Roy murmured. "Or it was back in my day. It's going to be tough to sneak up on with all that light."

Roy wasn't wrong. Albert could see how much open ground they needed to cover. Whether they made it undetected would come down to the attentiveness of the guards. He squinted at the guard hut next to the main gate. The small wooden box had contained a man when he passed through it earlier, there to operate the barrier. A second man was outside in the road to check the people coming in.

Now there was no sign of either man but staring at the small hut he caught the flare of a cigarette being lit just as a man opened the door and stepped out. The gates were closed, the barrier was down, and the guards could probably be counted on to pay no attention to activity inside the camp. If they chose their approach route carefully, they were unlikely to be seen.

"What about the cameras?" Roy asked, pointing where they were mounted on the edge of more than one building.

Albert chewed the inside of his cheek for a moment. If the cameras were recording, they would be in trouble. It was a gamble, but if they weren't he doubted there was a person in the world dedicated enough to watch a bank of TV screens when they could be reading a book or watching Netflix on a tablet.

"I think we risk it," he said.

Roy shrugged. "In for a penny …"

"We should go fast. Limit the time we are exposed."

Roy grinned. "Race you!" He set off without warning, leaving Albert to chase after him.

In Albert's head, they moved across the open ground with grace and coordination, flitting between shadows and remaining invisible. He recalled watching an episode of *The Six Million Dollar Man* where *Steve Austin* had to run fast enough that the cameras wouldn't be able to track him.

Glancing to his left, he caught sight of Roy and was forced to accept that the comparison wasn't a good one. Roy's knees cracked audibly as he hurried, the sound they made easily mistaken for a Morse Code message perhaps demanding to know why he was making them work so hard.

Nevertheless, they made it to the edge of the nearest building, Rex dancing and spinning in his excitement, without shouts of alarm or actual alarms wailing in the night to indicate they'd been spotted.

The building housed some of the camp's residents. They could tell because the sound of people snoring reached their ears despite the windows being shut tight to keep the cold out.

As they approached the main building, Albert spotted yet another security camera. It looked like it had been designed by the East Germans sometime before the wall came down. Ancient, but probably still functional. A bit like *The Rolling Stones*.

They edged along the row of buildings, creeping toward the one they wanted and doing their best to stay away from the cameras. Only now did it occur to Albert that the building might be locked. Not only that, the entrance was at the front of the building in direct sight of the front gates. Even if the other guards were asleep or paying no attention, the duo at the gate couldn't fail to see two old men and a large dog wandering into the Unlimited Horizons HQ.

So it was a mercy that Albert spotted an open window on the ground floor of the main building. Not only was it open, it was on the back face and in a shadow cast by a tall chimney. They would not be seen by anyone.

Albert gripped Roy's head, twisting it toward the open window until his friend saw it too. He got a thumbs up.

The window was only open a crack at the bottom, but with both of them pushing, it slid upwards easily enough.

"How do we do this?" Roy asked.

The window was at head height. Sixty years ago, either one of them could have jumped and sailed through the opening with minimal effort. Those days were long gone.

Albert looked around for something they could stand on. A handy stepladder tucked around the corner proved to be too much to hope for, but they found a wheelie bin and carefully manoeuvred it under the opening.

"Let's lift Rex up first," Albert suggested.

Rex's eyebrows twitched. "*Um, what?*"

"What does he weigh?" asked Roy, bending down to get his hands under the dog's belly and chest.

Albert didn't know, but said, "A lot. The fat git eats everything in sight."

Rex frowned. "*Excuse me?*" Any further comment was lost when the pensioners hoisted him into the air. He stepped onto the lid of the wheelie bin, clambered through the window and onto the sill before jumping down on the other side.

He found himself in an office. There were three desks with chairs on which three computers sat. Personal items both on the desks and in the drawers (Rex could smell breath mints and medicated tissues) suggested the office was in daily use. Had he been human, he might have described the scent profile as that of industrial-strength cleaning products and vague bureaucratic despair.

At the sound of laboured breathing and general protesting, Rex turned to find his human climbing through the window. Albert's leading hand slipped, spilling him to the carpet with a choice word or three.

Rex licked his face.

"Thank you, Rex," Albert pushed him away.

Roy joined him, crouching alongside Albert because he thought his friend was keeping low on purpose.

Once the pain in Albert's backside subsided, he got to his feet, using Rex as an anchor to pull on. The door to the office wasn't locked, and now they were inside with the freedom to roam.

Chapter 12

Albert needed only a few moments to orientate himself. They emerged from the office two doors along from the room where he first saw Horst Schultz addressing his latest intake. Retracing his steps, Albert found the foyer, the stairs, and then the mayor's office.

Yet again Albert was pleasantly surprised to find it unlocked. They were big on trust it seemed.

Inside the office, the curtains were pulled, most likely to keep the afternoon sun from blinding the mayor when he sat at his desk, but it meant darkness enveloped them like a clingy ex-partner and that played right into their hands.

Beams of torchlight swinging around would give them away in a heartbeat, but with the curtains shut they both produced the cheap, battery torches Beverly purchased at the same time as the wire cutters.

Roy clicked on his torch, keeping the beam pointed downward to minimize visibility from outside just in case. The office was exactly as Albert remembered it – ostentatious, pretentious, and with enough mahogany to make an environmentalist spontaneously combust.

Rex made a beeline for the door at the back of the office, pulled there by the same strange feline-but-not smell he detected the first time he came into the room. It was stronger on the other side of the door, but his human arrived before Rex could explore further.

"What is it, boy?" Albert whispered. He'd crossed the room to see if Rex had found something of interest, but the door led to a short corridor which ended at a locked door. Maybe there was something on the other side and maybe there wasn't. Albert had enough to look through in the mayor's office without breaking down doors just to see what might lie beyond.

"Come on, Rex," Albert clicked his tongue for Rex to follow and went back to help Roy explore.

Rex sniffed again. There was something about the smell that worried him. It was cat-like, but he could tell the creature leaving the scent behind wasn't an everyday moggie. Unable to go any further, he wandered back to the office to see what the humans were doing.

At the desk, Roy rifled through a pile of neatly stacked paperwork. It was his first time breaking and entering. His first time searching for clues in the middle of the night and he felt like *James Bond*. Before they set off, Albert gave him some tips about how and where to look, that they needed to be swift, and how it was in their best interest to leave everything as they found it.

While Roy inspected the items on the top of the desk, Albert turned his attention to the wastepaper basket. It contained several crumpled papers, an apple core, and a coffee cup. Enough to prove even cult leaders have surprisingly mundane trash.

Albert extracted the papers, smoothing them out on the carpet so he could hope to read them. Most were in German, and though he searched for words he might recognise, the underlying gist of what was written eluded him. Until he found a list of names, beside which were dates. The first Albert surmised to be the birthdate of the person named. They ranged from the mid-sixties all the way up to the late nineties. The second date was ... today, Albert realised.

Scrutinising the page more closely, he counted the names. There were thirty-two, the same number of people he found listening to Horst when he walked into his session. Annotated in pen next to some names were a few words in German. Not every name had them, but some did, and Albert knew enough German to be able to understand what he was seeing.

Rising from the carpet into a kneeling position, Albert placed the page on the desk.

"Roy, have a look at this."

Roy abandoned the pile of papers he'd been looking through, his furrowed brow continuing to question something he'd seen a few moments earlier.

"I think these are the people I saw here yesterday. They looked like new arrivals. Horst was lecturing them about the whole digital ascension thing. Preaching might be a better word. Right here," Albert pointed to the ink notes by some of the names, "Arzt is the German word for doctor. Lehrer is a teacher, and I think Anwalt is a lawyer."

"Why is he identifying what they do?"

Albert had no idea, but said, "It was clearly important enough for Herr Schultz to want to write it down." He folded the sheet of paper and tucked it into his pocket. "Did you find anything?"

Roy went back to the pile of paper. "Only this." He leafed through the inch thick stack to find what he was looking for. I thought it was nothing at the time, but I've just worked out what BTC is."

Albert gave him a blank look.

"It's Bitcoin. At least, I think it is."

Albert had heard of the cryptocurrency, but how it worked, what it looked like, and how a person then spent it was completely beyond his comprehension. He looked at the page Roy had found. It contained a series of alphanumeric strings, followed by amounts in Euros, with a handwritten note at the bottom: Transfer complete. 50 BTC = €2.4M. Next extraction scheduled for Friday.

"That's not chump change," Roy pointed out.

Albert picked out the sheet, carefully folded the paper, and placed it in his pocket where it joined his handkerchief and some mints that were old enough to vote.

They looked for a while longer but failed to turn up anything else of interest. Checking his watch, Albert was surprised to discover more than an hour had passed since they snuck through the fence.

"We should go," he said.

Before Roy could respond, Rex's ears pricked up. Someone was coming. He could hear their feet on the stairs.

Albert saw his dog's hackles rise moments before he heard voices.

"I'm telling you I saw something," came a man's voice in the hallway outside.

"Yeah. Like the time you thought you saw that hot Sabrina chick getting undressed in her office and wanted to see if she was okay. Or the time you thought you saw someone sneaking through the woods and had us all out searching for three hours."

"I did see someone!" snapped the first voice.

Like escaping POWs trying to evade a searchlight, Roy and Albert knew they were about to be caught. The only place they could go was through the door at the back of the office, but there was no time to get there. If they ran, their footsteps would give them away. The only place in the whole office that offered them the opportunity to hide was the …

"Under the desk!" hissed Albert diving for cover like a man who's just spotted his wife entering a restaurant where he's dining with his new girlfriend.

Grabbing Rex, he stuffed himself into the space between the drawers on either side. Had the desk not been so big and imposing they wouldn't have fit. As it was, they all had to squeeze in and breathe shallow.

The light flicked on, illuminating the room and their poor life choices in equal measure. From their hiding place, they could see nothing. The solid wood came all the way to the carpet and the drawers to their left and right encapsulated them completely. However, should the guard choose to walk around to peer behind the desk, they would be as caught as a squirrel in a vending machine.

The newcomer moved farther into the room, stopping directly at the desk. Papers rustled above their heads. Albert didn't dare breathe. He had one hand on his dog's tail in case Rex felt like wagging it, and his heartbeat was so loud he was convinced it would register on the Richter scale.

"See? No one here. Can we go now? We're not supposed to leave the front gate unguarded. Ever."

There was enough impatience in the voice to give Albert hope. He was contorted into a position that was going to play havoc with his back if he didn't move soon. Eyes closed, he prayed the guards were about to leave.

"Hans! Come on!"

Reluctantly, and with a whine, the guard in the room accepted defeat and walked away. The light went out, they heard footsteps retreating down the hallway, but neither man moved until the voices faded away.

"That was a close one," Roy murmured, spilling from the cavity under the desk to collapse on the floor.

Rex followed him out. "*Humans are really strange sometimes, you know that?*"

Unfolding himself, Albert crawled into free space, used the desk to lever himself off the carpet, and got to his feet.

"Perhaps it's time we called it a night."

Roy agreed.

They peered cautiously around the door frame, just to be certain the guards hadn't double bluffed them only to wait at the end of the corridor. With no sound or sight of anyone, they made their way back to the office through which they entered the building. The wheelie bin was still where they left it. Escaping the compound and returning to the hotel was going to be a simple reversal of the process to get in.

Except it wasn't.

Halfway through the window, one leg perched on the lid of the wheelie bin, Albert's hands slipped. He fell, his panicked fingers scrambling to grasp anything that would alleviate his fall. What his right hand found was the lid of the wheelie bin. They had pushed it against the building with the open edge to the window, so as he fell, he pulled the bin lid open. Roy, lunging to catch his friend before he fell, missed and pitched headfirst into the bin's dark interior with a loud thud when he hit the bottom.

That it was empty might have been a relief at any other time, but in the compound's quiet interior, the sound he made trying to get out again was like a tumbling one-man band falling down a particularly long set of stairs.

Helping Roy to his feet, Albert dispensed with all sense of subtlety and stealth. "I think we need a new plan!"

"Yeah! Got one?"

"I do!" said Albert. "Leg it!"

Chapter 13

With Rex bounding along beside them, Albert and Roy ran for the trees, the chill of the night air hitting them like a refreshing slap of reality.

"Which way?" Roy gasped.

Albert pointed toward the tree line. "Back the way we came!" They could lose the guards in the dense woods where it would be hard to follow on anything motorised. Bruno and Thomas made it through on their dirt bikes, but not the way Albert and Roy came. That was a different part of the fence.

They wouldn't need dirt bikes to catch them, though. Albert and Roy were going as fast as they could, but that wasn't saying much, and they knew it. The *Steve Austin* image played through Albert's head again. He remembered watching it with Gary. His eldest was young enough in the 70's to sit on daddy's lap while the *Six Million Dollar Man* faked running fast by going in slow motion. That was how they looked now – like they would be overtaking cars if someone would just play the film at the right speed.

Leaving no doubt in their minds, shouts from the guards at the front gate confirmed they were being pursued. How many other armed guards there might be they couldn't guess, but Albert imagined a squad of them pouring from a building like angry wasps swarming from a disturbed nest.

Rex kept pace with the humans by maintaining a steady trot. He checked behind them a few times, noting the relative position of the two men he could see in pursuit. They would catch up, that much was certain, but Rex planned to intercept them long before that happened.

His plan changed just as they reached the trees.

Albert didn't need to see them to know the Dobermanns were giving chase. He heard their deep, threatening barks and spared a glance at Roy. Neither had the breath to say anything. All they could do was keep moving. They'd heard someone shouting into a radio and expected to find forces converging on their position. When Albert did flick a glance over his shoulder, just before the darkness of the woods swallowed him, he saw the camp's residents filtering from their accommodation looking sleepy and bewildered.

The woods were darker than the inside of a coal mine at midnight, which would have been brilliant for hiding if not for the minor inconvenience of not being able to see where they were going. Albert collided with a low-hanging branch that seemed to have been positioned specifically to catch him in the forehead.

The barking behind them grew louder and more frenzied. The Dobermans were gaining ground with relentless efficiency.

They were at least a hundred yards from the fence and the chances they would find it at the exact spot they came through were slim. That didn't really matter, though, because they would be caught long before they could reach it.

Panting breathlessly, Albert looked around for Rex. He wanted to tell him to go ahead. If Rex could get out, he could find Beverly and Mila. He wouldn't be able to explain what happened, but they would figure it out by themselves.

But Rex wasn't there. Had he been, he would have said something like, "*Hold my beer,*" before refusing to obey his human's command and reversing course to deal with the imminent threat. As it was, Rex had already accepted the Dobermans would catch the humans long before they got to the fence and had stopped to tackle the problem.

The Dobermans burst through the undergrowth, their sleek bodies designed for speed and intimidation. They skidded to a halt when they spotted Rex standing his ground, clearly surprised by this unexpected show of canine defiance.

"*Well, well,*" growled Hades, the larger of the two. "*If it isn't the trespassing mutt again.*"

"*Back for more trouble,*" added Cerberus, circling to Rex's left with the subtlety of a politician avoiding a direct question.

Rex remained completely unimpressed. "*I see they've let you off your leads again. Did they remember to give you your thinking brains this time, or are you still operating on factory settings?*"

The Dobermans exchanged confused glances. This was not the response they were accustomed to receiving from terrified intruders.

"*We are guard dogs,*" snarled Hades, emphasizing each syllable as if explaining quantum physics to a particularly dense individual. "*This is our territory.*"

"*Is it though?*" Rex tilted his head with exaggerated curiosity. "*Do you own it? Can you sell it? Do you get to decide who comes and goes? Or are you just the unpaid security staff who get thrown biscuits when you perform tricks for the humans?*"

This philosophical inquiry clearly wasn't what the Dobermans had prepared for. Cerberus shook his head as if trying to dislodge Rex's questions.

"*We don't need to own it,*" he growled, though with slightly less conviction. "*We protect it.*"

"*Protect it from what, exactly?*" Rex asked, sitting down as if they were having a pleasant chat over afternoon tea. "*You realize you're guarding something dodgy, right? Or are your brains as empty as tennis balls?*"

The Dobermans, suddenly remembering their purpose, made to dash past Rex, but he moved to his right, unleashing the low branch he'd pushed backward with his body almost to the point where it would break. Released, the branch whipped back to its original position, carving a silent path through the air that took out all eight Doberman legs before they even saw it coming.

Rex didn't like that he was forced to hurt them, but it was for their own good and he couldn't allow them to catch the humans in his pack.

Standing over the felled black and tan dogs as they whined in pain, he barked, "*Not so fast, flea hotels. We're having a conversation here. It's called manners. Though I wouldn't expect you to know about those, given that you chase people through woods for a living.*"

"*The humans will reward us,*" Hades insisted, though he made no attempt to get up. His legs hurt and he feared the German Shepherd might yet have other tricks to unleash.

"*With what? Extra kibble? A slightly softer blanket in your kennel?*" Rex snorted. "*Meanwhile, they're taking advantage of vulnerable humans. The strong dogs look after the weaker members of the pack. But sure, you keep wagging your tails for the scraps they throw you.*"

Something in Rex's words seemed to connect, however faintly. The Dobermans' aggressive posture softened almost imperceptibly.

"*What do you mean?*" Cerberus asked, his ears twitching with reluctant curiosity.

Rex was about to elaborate on this promising opening when a new scent caught his attention. It was the smell from the mayor's office, but no longer contained and distant. It was here, it was close, and it was … big.

The Dobermans sensed it too and their demeanour changed instantly, from confident predators to nervous subordinates. Getting to their paws, they backed away, heads lowered submissively.

"*He's here*," whispered Hades, all bravado gone from his voice.

"*Who's here?*" Rex asked, though the hackles rising along his spine suggested his instincts already knew the answer.

"*Raven*," Cerberus whimpered. "*The master's cat.*"

Chapter 14

"*Cat?*" Rex scoffed. "*What kind of cat has you two quivering like puppies in a thunderstorm?*"

His question was answered by a low, rumbling growl that seemed to emanate from the darkness itself. It was the kind of sound that bypassed the conscious brain and went straight to the primal part that recognizes when something large and hungry is considering you for dinner.

From the shadows emerged a shape that redefined Rex's understanding of the word 'cat'. This wasn't some fluffy tabby chasing string or a grumpy Siamese demanding food. This was nature's perfect killing machine – a panther, its coat darker than the night around it, its yellow eyes gleaming with predatory intelligence.

The moonlight seemed to shy away, avoiding the dangerous animal as though scared to touch it.

"*Oh,*" Rex managed, his usual witty repartee temporarily replaced by stunned silence.

The panther regarded him with the cold, calculating stare of something that views the world as divided into two simple categories: things it can eat, and things it can beat. Rex doubted it mattered into which group he fell. The panther was at least his size and almost certainly stronger. That was a problem, but not nearly so concerning as the claws he felt sure the cat would have at the end of each giant paw.

Finding his gumption, Rex addressed the Dobermans without taking his eyes off the panther, "*So you two take orders from a cat?*"

"*It's not like we have a lot of choice,*" Hades muttered.

"*Raven does what the master says,*" added Cerberus, "*and we do what Raven says.*"

In stopping to face the dogs, Rex intended only to delay them. Had he known about the panther, he might have devised a different strategy, but he believed he'd bought enough time for the humans to reach the fence and now it was time to follow.

Backing away, he said, "*Well, it's been lovely chatting, but I think my human might be missing me.*"

The panther growled again, this time lower and more threatening, and it crouched, muscles tensing beneath its sleek coat.

"*I don't suppose you'd consider a philosophical discussion about the nature of territorial boundaries and the social contract?*" Rex tried, backing away another step.

The panther's only response was to begin slinking forward, its movements so fluid it appeared to be gliding rather than walking.

"*Right. Didn't think so.*" Rex turned and ran. Behind him, he could hear the panther in pursuit, its paws hitting the ground in a rhythm that was terrifyingly fast and eerily quiet.

Albert and Roy were in sight of the fence when Rex came bounding toward them.

Eyes wide, scarcely able to believe they were still fumbling around on this side of it, Rex barked, "*Run faster, you idiots!*"

Relief at seeing his dog return, vanished the next moment, when fear kicked it firmly in the teeth. Albert had been about to ask why Rex was barking so madly when he saw the panther streak through the night like a shadow in pursuit of his canine companion.

"Good Lord!" Roy exclaimed.

"The fence!" Albert shouted. By chance or miracle, the cut section they came through was to their right. With the huge black cat coming their way, it formed a beacon of hope in their woodland odyssey of terror. Roy reached it first, his fingers scrabbling at the wire to pull it open.

Rex glanced over his shoulder to find the panther gaining on him with the unhurried confidence of a predator that knows its prey can't possibly escape.

"Come on, boy!" Albert called, his voice tight with fear. He was halfway through the fence and ready to pull it shut the moment his dog landed safe on the other side.

Rex put on a final burst of speed, but the panther was simply too fast for him. Just as Rex reached the fence, the panther slammed into his hindquarters, sending him tumbling into the steel mesh. He hit the fence, missed the hole, and bounced off.

Knowing it would be folly to tackle the powerful cat, Albert tried to get back through the hole anyway, and would have made it had Roy not grabbed his arm.

"Let me go!" Albert demanded, trying to yank his arm free.

"I can't let you do that, old boy."

"Rex is in trouble!"

"And he's moving too fast for you to help." Roy's words were soothing and apologetic. They were also correct. Rex and the panther were already gone. Unable to get to his human and safety, Rex put his head down and ran.

He was in blind flight mode for perhaps the first time in his life. Oh, he'd come up against other dogs he didn't want to fight, and on more than one occasion had elected to run when facing a gang of cats, but never had he felt so gripped by terror.

If he lost in a fight to a dog, he might limp away with a few injuries and need a day or three to feel himself again. Lose to the panther and Rex knew there was a chance he wouldn't walk away at all.

He needed a strategy, but he didn't have one. The cat was stronger, faster, and more dangerous. Cornering hard around the trunk of a tree, he heard the cat growl its displeasure at missing the chance to take him down.

Rex knew his only hope lay on the other side of the fence. Only by placing a barrier between himself and the panther could he hope to survive. With that in mind, he ducked a low branch, turned hard around the next tree, and felt the muscles in his left rear leg go numb when one of the panther's mighty paws swatted it.

His back legs tangled, and he fell, unable to stop the inevitable crunch as his out-of-control body slammed into the ground. Inertia caused his body to roll, and luck stepped in to save him from a death blow.

The panther was in the air, leaping to land on the dog with a plan to bite the back of his neck. He would sink his teeth in and hold on, using his claws to keep the German Shepherd in place until he succumbed to the inevitable. However, he came down on top of Rex at the exact moment he had all his paws in the air. Rex hadn't planned the defensive move, but the cat landed on his legs and flew away to the right as Rex's rolling body passed the energy from one to the other.

When the sudden weight pushed him down, Rex slid another foot and rolled back onto his paws. Wasting no time, he drove off with his powerful back legs and raced for the fence once more. If he was going to get a chance to escape, this was it.

Having seen his dog vanish into the woodland, all Albert could do was watch and wait. He could track Rex's movement through the undergrowth, but it was far too dark to see anything.

Until Rex emerged into a patch of moonlight, his head down and his fur flowing.

"Come on, boy! That's it!" Albert had stepped back through the hole in the fence, leaving Roy on the other side ready to push the steel mesh closed. They had found a chunky branch to seal the gap. It wouldn't hold forever, but all they had to do was get away.

The Dobermans were off to one side, unsure what they were supposed to do. They knew they ought to chase and tackle the two old humans, but Rex made some valid points and they were confused about where their loyalties should lie. Were they being mistreated by the humans? Should they be taking orders from a cat?

Rex, focused solely on his human and the gap in the fence, pushed as hard as he could. He'd left the panther behind but wasn't fooled into thinking he could slow down. This was as much a race for survival as it had ever been.

Exploding through a bush, the enraged panther hit the ground a few yards behind the fleeing German Shepherd.

Behind Albert, Roy swore under his breath.

Albert felt a tap on his arm and turned to see Roy offering him something.

"Here. Take this." It was his sword. It was out of its sheath and gleamed when the moonlight caught the edge of the razor-sharp blade.

His expression grim, Albert stepped back through the gap holding the sword in both hands. If he needed to kill the black cat, so be it. He wasn't about to let it hurt Rex.

Ten yards to go. Eight. With each pace Rex ate up the distance between the panther and safety, but he still wasn't fast enough.

The panther swatted at his rear flank again, trying the same trick intended to bring the dog down for a second time. It worked, Rex's legs tangling once more, but instead of rolling, he skidded forward on his chest with his front and back legs splayed.

The giant cat landed on his rump, sinking claws and teeth into his back end.

Rex howled in pain and tried to get up.

Hades and Cerberus watched. They'd seen the panther in action before and knew the German Shepherd was done for. Fear that the same could so easily be their fate was what kept them in line. The cat had only one weakness that they knew of and though they believed it could be exploited, they could devise no strategy that would benefit them in the long run.

The panther grinned victoriously. It could taste blood. Not a lot, it had barely punctured the dog's skin, but now that it was down, all he needed was to change position and deliver the death blow. It was going to be easy.

"Get off him!" Albert screamed the words and stabbed the sword into the panther's hide. He didn't want to hurt it. Not really. The panther was just an animal. None of this was its fault. Had it been left in its natural habitat it would hunt and breed and be able to live its normal natural life. For that reason, his strike was intended to wound rather than kill, but it did the trick.

The panther squealed in pain, leaping from the dog to get away from the searing agony in its shoulder.

The moment Rex was no longer pinned to the ground, Albert yanked hold of a handful of loose fur and pulled.

Rex needed no such encouragement.

From the other side of the fence, Roy shouted, "Come on!"

Man and dog, racing for safety, tumbled through the gap to sprawl in the leaf litter and dirt on the other side. Ready with the branch, Roy threaded it through the two sides and turned like he was applying a tourniquet.

The fence now secure, Albert, Roy and Rex stared through it to the animals on the other side and the stillness of the woodland returned.

Panting about as hard as he ever had, Rex was glad of the cold air. It would help him to get his body temperature under control. The panther was back on its feet and looked mad. Its bottom jaw hung open enough to show the rows of deadly teeth.

Roy stood over Albert, offering a hand to help him up. They gripped forearms and balanced each other to haul Albert from the ground.

Back on his feet, Albert said, "Come along, Rex. Let's go. I want to take a look at your wounds."

The puncture marks from the panther's teeth and claws were painful, but Rex knew they were not all that bad. Not really. He'd survived but didn't like the idea of a rematch. The panther wasn't saying anything, but that was okay, for Rex's parting comment was aimed at the guard dogs.

Narrowing his eyes at them, Rex said, "*This is who you obey? A cat and a bunch of criminals? We are dogs. We are better than this. You are better than this.*"

Limping ever so slightly, Rex turned around and walked away.

Chapter 15

Albert led Roy and Rex along a different route back to the hotel. Following the fence back to the road was the logical course of action and the shortest route, but convinced the guards would be looking for them around the camp's perimeter, they headed through the woods instead.

Rex limped alongside his human. His injuries were superficial, but his pride was severely damaged.

"*Cat beats dog*," Rex muttered, his ears dropping as he trekked through the undergrowth. "*That's not how the natural order is supposed to work.*"

When they finally emerged onto a road, Albert breathed a sigh of relief to find their meandering route through the woods hadn't deviated too far. The petrol station at the edge of town was just to their right. They watched for several minutes, gauging as best they could whether someone might be watching. Eventually, though, they had to hope for the best and cross the road.

If guards from the camp were looking for them, this was the most dangerous time. It was after two in the morning. The town was asleep, the roads deserted, and the three figures moving through the streets were the only signs of life. They'd been seen inside the camp, that much they were sure of, but only from a distance. The guards never made it to the fence to catch them escaping. They sent the dogs instead and someone released the panther.

Horst Schultz would receive the report and know it was them. Even from a distance, the guards would have been able to tell they were seeing two old men and a large dog.

"Are you all right?" Albert asked, putting a hand on Rex's head and scratching behind his ears. The dog had saved them earlier, intercepting the Dobermans so he and Roy could reach the fence.

Rex wagged his tail half-heartedly, the effort clearly causing him some pain.

"We'll get you patched up as soon as we get back," Albert promised.

"I need to make a confession, old boy," Roy said. "I didn't expect we'd find anything tonight. I thought it would be fun, and don't get me wrong, Albert, I know you know what you are doing when it comes to investigating someone. But I still expected it to be something of a wild goose chase that would end with Beverly saying, 'I told you so' for the next three decades."

Albert smiled. "And now?"

"Now I don't know what to think." Roy's face was hard to make out in the darkness, but the set of his jaw was grim. "That operation is not on the level, Albert. Not by a long shot."

"No," Albert agreed. "It isn't."

They walked in silence for a while, each lost in his own thoughts. Albert's mind was racing, trying to make sense of what they'd discovered. The list of names, the Bitcoin transaction. He could do some research to improve what he knew about cryptocurrency but would need to consult his kids to understand what kind of crimes could be committed with it.

The hotel came into view, the twin lights either side of the front door a welcome sight. Albert felt a surge of relief. His body ached. He was getting a bit long in the tooth for running, let alone clambering through windows and diving around on the ground.

Beverly appeared in the corridor, emerging from Albert's/Mila's room when she heard footsteps.

Her expression was one of anger, but it quickly softened when she saw the state of the returning trio.

"Let's get you all inside," she ushered them through the door.

Mila looked like she'd been sleeping and was wiping her eyes and yawning when Albert came into the room.

"Rex is hurt," she observed, concern in her voice.

Rex slumped to the carpet, head on his front paws and thankful to be able to stop moving.

"*Yup*," he said. "*It's not a big deal. I just need some sleep.*" He closed his eyes, ready to go to sleep, then snapped them open again and lifted his head. "*Unless there's a gravy bone available.*"

Beverly fetched a first aid kit she had with her in case of emergencies. It was a small, travel accessory she'd bought years earlier, but it had served its purpose enough times to justify carrying it.

All attention turned to Rex as Albert inspected his flanks and hindquarters. He found the puncture wounds easily enough, making Rex wince and whine when he touched them.

Beverly tutted and worried but got busy with cream and gauze strips to clean the holes and scratches.

Above the dog, the humans talked.

Anxious to learn something, Mila knew she ought to ask about what they found and how the dog came to be wounded, but she couldn't stop herself from asking the question she really wanted to know.

"Did you find my sister?"

Roy said, "I'm afraid not, my dear. We didn't see anyone until the very end, and we were running away by then."

Interrupting their guests before she could ask a second question, Beverly asked, "What happened to Rex? These look like bite marks."

"Ah, yes, well, we had a bit of a run-in with some local wildlife," Roy replied, trying for casual nonchalance and missing.

"Wildlife?" Beverly echoed. She wasn't buying it for a second. "What kind of wildlife leaves puncture wounds like these?" She parted Rex's fur to point out one of the tooth holes in his butt.

"The extremely large and bitey kind," Roy admitted.

"It was a panther," Albert explained. Standing up, he removed his coat and hung it over the back of a chair. "The mayor keeps a panther as a pet. It doesn't take kindly to intruders."

"A panther?" Beverly eyed her husband with severe doubt, then switched her gaze to check with Albert. Her husband found it fun to deceive her with wild tales he would later laughingly admit were utter fabrications, but Albert wasn't so childish. Seeing his expression, she looked back down at Rex's wound and mumbled, "Wow."

Mila shook her head. "I heard rumours about a panther, but I thought they were just silly stories. I never thought they could be true."

"Well," said Albert, "they are." While Beverly cleaned Rex's wounds, he extracted the papers from his pocket and laid them on the small hotel desk. They were crumpled but still legible.

"What are those?" Mila asked, moving to look over his shoulder.

"Evidence, I think. I'm just not sure what they are evidence of," Albert replied, smoothing the sheets. "This one is a list of names. I found it in the mayor's office. I think they are the people who arrived yesterday." He pointed to the date. "And this one," he tapped the second sheet, "shows a Bitcoin transaction worth over two million euros."

Mila's eyes widened. "Two million? What are they doing with that kind of money?"

"That, my dear," Albert said, "is the two point four-million-euro question."

Beverly, having finished cleaning Rex's wounds, joined them at the desk. "Let me see." She put on her reading glasses and peered at the list of names. "There must be thirty people here."

"Thirty-two," Albert corrected. "I counted them."

"And what are these notes?" she asked, pointing to the handwritten annotations beside some of the names.

"That's their professions," Albert explained. "Doctor, teacher, lawyer ... Horst seems particularly interested in people with certain credentials."

Rex, patched up and feeling marginally better, wandered over to join the huddle. He sat beside Albert, leaning against his leg for support.

Albert fought to make sense of what he knew so far, but the crimes, if that was what they were seeing, were far outside his field of expertise. Unlimited Horizons recruited people by offering them safety, sanctuary, a life free of digital binds, but what then? They surrendered their identity and lived in the community Mayor Horst ran as its facilitator. So how did they pay for food and energy? There had to be an income underpinning the camp and its residents. And what was the Bitcoin thing all about? The handwritten note at the bottom of the sheet of paper suggested the money was going out – being 'extracted'. Were they taking money from the residents as part of their digital ascension?

"Mila, when you went into the camp, did they ask you to surrender any money? Bank savings, that sort of thing?"

Mila frowned, thinking for a moment before saying, "No. Money was never discussed."

"But they took your bank cards?" Albert continued the line of questioning.

Shock registered on Mila's face. "Oh, my God! Do you think they might have taken my money?" She was up and moving, crossing the room to the bed where Beverly's laptop sat dormant.

Roy touched Albert's arm to get his attention. "What are you thinking, old boy?"

"That feeding, housing, and caring for people costs money. The upkeep of the camp, wages for the staff, unless we think the guards are doing it for free, all costs money. If people coming in surrender everything tying them to the outside world, surely that includes their money."

"But how would they get it?" Beverly questioned, sounding doubtful. "They wouldn't have the login codes and it's not like they can walk into a bank and make a withdrawal. You need identification and bank cards …" her voice trailed off.

"That's right," Albert nodded. "They have all those things, and they don't need to look like the real person. They can forge new identities using what they have."

Mila swore. Loudly. And swore again. The words were in her native tongue, but it was easy enough to understand what she was saying.

"They took the lot!" she raged. "I didn't have much, but every last penny is gone."

Albert drew in a long, slow breath. It was what he expected her to discover, but worried they were only seeing the tip of the iceberg. Maybe the combined sums would add up to a few million, especially with doctors and lawyers involved, but the note said, 'next extraction scheduled for next Friday.' It was less than a week away, so they were mining millions a week and that didn't add up.

They were missing something.

Rex whined softly, sensing the tension in the room. Albert absentmindedly scratched the dog's ear, his mind racing ahead.

"We need more information," he decided. "We have part of the picture, but not all of it. Tomorrow, we need to look deeper into Sabrina Aldridge, the mayor, Unlimited Horizons, and these Bitcoin transactions."

"I can help with the online research," Beverly offered, surprising everyone. In response to their startled looks, she added, "What? I'm not completely useless with computers. I manage our online banking, don't I, Roy?"

"That you do, my dear," Roy agreed.

Feeling the weight of the day pressing down on him, Albert knew he was exhausted and could see the others were too. Rex had already laid down on the carpet, his eyes drooping.

"We should get some rest," he said. "It's late, and we've got a busy day ahead of us tomorrow."

"Understatement of the century," Roy muttered. "We've just broken into a cult compound, stolen documents, faced down guard dogs, and escaped a panther who was about as friendly as an angry chainsaw."

Roy summed things up nicely. They were poking a hornet's nest with a particularly short stick, and it was only a matter of time before the buzzing turned into a full-scale attack.

"Where will you sleep?" Mila asked Albert, gesturing around what was supposed to be his room.

"I'll bunk with Roy," Albert replied. "If that's all right with you two?"

Beverly nodded. Roy gave her a hug and a kiss before following Albert from the room.

When Rex moved to follow, Albert said, "No, boy. You stay here and guard the ladies. Okay?"

It was a task Rex recognised and understood. Placing his head back on the carpet, he was asleep before his human left the room.

Chapter 16

Albert woke to the sound of Roy snoring like a bear gargling marbles through a microphone. He checked his watch. It was just past eight in the morning, which meant he'd managed about five hours of sleep. It wasn't enough, but it would do. He was awake and knew Rex would want his breakfast.

His back protested as he rolled to his side and sat up on the edge of the bed. It had been a long time since ... No, Albert decided, he'd never spent a night in bed next to a man. At least, not since he was a small child and he couldn't recall doing it then either.

Roy rolled over, mumbled something incomprehensible, and continued his symphony of snores, completely unbothered by Albert's movements.

After a quick shower and a change of clothes, Albert headed down to the hotel's small breakfast room. He planned to get a hot drink and send a text to Roy's wife. He wanted to check on Rex, but everyone had been late to bed, so knocking on the door and waking them felt cruel. However, Beverly was already there, nursing a cup of tea and looking remarkably fresh for someone who had been up so late the previous night.

"Good morning," she greeted him. "The coffee's not bad."

Albert smiled and poured himself a cup. "How's Rex this morning?"

"Still asleep, sprawled across the carpet like he owns the place," Beverly reported. "I checked his wounds before I came down. They're not infected, but he'll be sore for a few days."

Albert nodded gratefully. "And Mila?"

"She's still asleep too. Poor girl was exhausted."

They sat in companionable silence for a few minutes, Albert savouring the surprisingly decent coffee. His mind was already working on the day ahead, mentally listing the steps they needed to take to unravel the mystery of Unlimited Horizons.

"Mr Smith?" The hotel manager appeared at his elbow. He was a thin, nervous-looking man in his forties with a receding hairline and glasses that seemed too big for his face. "Excuse me, Mr Smith?"

Albert looked up. "Yes?"

"There is a police officer here to see you." He glanced nervously over one shoulder, looking on edge to have the authorities on his premises so early in the day. "He asks that you join him in the lobby."

Albert and Beverly exchanged glances. They'd skirted around the subject last night when he, Rex, and Roy returned, but Albert wasn't surprised to hear the police wanted to speak with him.

"Tell him I'll be right there," Albert replied calmly.

The manager nodded and scurried away, looking relieved to have completed his task without incident.

"Should I wake Roy?" Beverly asked, her voice low.

Albert considered the question for a moment, then shook his head. "Not yet. Let's see what they want first." He left Beverly behind to observe and report if necessary. Albert doubted he was about to get arrested – if that was their plan they would have executed it already – but it wasn't beyond the realms of possibility that they would decide to do so after questioning him.

In the lobby waited a tall, broad-shouldered man in a police uniform. His silver hair was cut short in a military style, and he stood with the rigid posture of someone who viewed slouching as a personal failing. The nameplate on his uniform read 'Kramer'. Albert was familiar enough with foreign insignia to tell the man was a senior rank if not the top man for the area.

"Mr Smith," he said, extending a hand. "I am Chief of Police Gerhard Kramer. Thank you for seeing me."

Albert shook the offered hand, noting the firm grip. "Chief Kramer. What can I do for you?"

Kramer glanced around the lobby, which was empty apart from the manager hovering nervously behind the reception desk.

"Perhaps we could speak somewhere more private?" Kramer suggested. His English was excellent, with only the slightest hint of an accent.

Albert nodded toward a small seating area in a corner of the lobby. It wasn't completely private, but it was far enough from the reception desk that their conversation wouldn't be overheard.

Once they were seated, Kramer wasted no time getting to the point. "Mr Smith, I understand you have been making inquiries about Mayor Schultz and his organisation, Unlimited Horizons."

Albert kept his face carefully neutral. "I've heard of them, yes."

"And you met with the mayor yesterday afternoon, I believe?"

"I did. Though 'met' might be stretching things. I was taken there by two of your officers without so much as an explanation."

Kramer's mouth twitched in what might have been amusement, but his eyes remained cold. "Yes, the mayor can be enthusiastic about meeting people of note. He mentioned you had an interesting conversation."

"Did he?" Albert replied. "And what else did the mayor mention?" The conversation appeared to have no direction, but he wasn't fooled. They were two boxers at the start of a fight, sizing each other up and waiting for the other to throw the first punch.

Kramer studied Albert for a long moment before continuing. "He also mentioned that there was an incident at the compound last night. A break-in."

And there it was. The real reason for Chief of Police Kramer's visit.

"Really?" Albert raised his eyebrows, the picture of innocent surprise. "That's concerning. Was anything taken?"

"Some papers, apparently. Nothing of great value." Kramer's gaze never left Albert's face. "The intruders were spotted but escaped before they could be apprehended."

"That's fortunate. For the intruders, I mean."

"Indeed." Kramer's smile didn't reach his eyes. "Most fortunate, considering they encountered the mayor's pet. It can be quite territorial."

Albert met the police chief's gaze steadily. "A pet, you say? What kind of pet would that be?"

"A large cat. Exotic. The mayor has special permits."

"How interesting. I've always been more of a dog person myself."

"Yes, I believe you have a German Shepherd. Rex, isn't it?" Kramer glanced around. "I don't see him with you this morning."

"He's resting. Strained his leg yesterday."

Kramer nodded slowly. "Walking in the woods can be hazardous. Uneven ground, hidden obstacles …"

"Large cats," Albert added.

The ghost of a smile crossed Kramer's face, gone so quickly Albert almost missed it. The police chief shifted in his seat, leaning forward slightly.

"Mr Smith, let me be direct. You are a visitor to our town, and an honoured one at that. Your reputation precedes you." His voice was smooth, but there was an edge to it, like a knife wrapped in silk. "However, Hoffenholen is a peaceful place. We value our tranquillity."

"That's understandable," Albert replied. "Most people do."

"Then perhaps you understand why it would concern me to discover those same honoured visitors start asking questions about our mayor and a few hours later someone breaks into a community on private property." Kramer's voice dropped to little more than a whisper.

"I would be concerned about that too," Albert said evenly. "If I knew anything about it."

Kramer sighed, leaning back in his chair. "Mr Smith, we both know that proving who was at the compound last night will be difficult. The security cameras are outdated, the witnesses' descriptions are vague, and the mayor is reluctant to make a formal complaint that might attract unwanted attention."

"How thoughtful of him."

"Mayor Schultz *is* a thoughtful man. He has done a great deal for this community." Kramer's tone took on a reverential quality. "After the military base closed, this town nearly died. The mayor's organisation brought jobs and purpose back to Hoffenholen."

Albert noted the shift in Kramer's demeanour. The man wasn't just following orders or protecting a powerful local figure – he genuinely believed in Horst Schultz.

"That's admirable," Albert said carefully. "Though I've heard some concerning things about his methods."

Kramer's expression hardened. "Rumours and misunderstandings, spread by those who fail to grasp the importance of his work. Unlimited Horizons helps people who struggle to survive amidst the toxic influences of modern life. It gives them purpose, community."

"And what happens to their possessions? Their money? Their identities?"

Kramer's eyes narrowed. "They are surrendered willingly as part of the process the mayor calls digital ascension. Legal documents are signed. Everything is above board."

Albert nodded thoughtfully. "I see. And the Bitcoin transactions? Are those above board too?"

For the first time, Kramer looked genuinely surprised. The reaction was brief – a widening of the eyes, a slight parting of the lips – but it was enough to tell Albert that the police chief wasn't privy to every aspect of the mayor's operation.

"I suspect you have been misled, Mr Smith. I believe you have a former member of the community staying with you. A former member who was disgruntled with how the camp is run."

The statement confirmed they knew where Mila was. Again, it wasn't a surprise. Albert suspected the police chief had been briefed by the mayor and was told to think of Mila as a bad influence and a troublemaker who came to the camp under false pretences.

"Mila is looking for her sister. She is concerned about her. She joined Unlimited Horizons to find her and was prevented from doing so. Why is that?"

Chief Kramer shifted in his chair as though uncomfortable but smiled and Albert saw his error. The question was one the other man expected and was ready to answer.

"As I understand it, the process of digital ascension is a complicated one that involves many stages and suffers if interrupted. Are you aware that the sister in question was an alcoholic and drug addict when she arrived here five months ago and is now free of both vices? Do you think she is being ill-treated, Mr Smith?"

"That fails to answer my question about Bitcoin, Chief Kramer. And if Talia is in such good health now, why is it that she is still prevented from seeing her sister? A sister who travelled across Europe to find her, tracking her all the way to the Unlimited Horizons camp."

"Come now, Mr Smith," the chief of police frowned. "You make it sound like Mila had to walk here with her luggage on her back. She arrived on a plane. Unlimited Horizons, so far as I can see, welcomed her with open arms. Had she stayed the course she might be with her sister now. Instead, she tried to break into the camp's restricted areas and subsequently ran away, finding you in the process. Doesn't it strike you as strange that so soon after she was caught where she shouldn't be that a second break in occurred?"

Yet again, Chief Kramer had shifted the conversation away from the subject of cryptocurrency. Albert wondered whether he was doing it deliberately and under instruction from the mayor, or by accident because he just didn't know anything about it.

Already on dodgy ground, Albert chose to throw caution to the wind.

"Are you involved?" he asked flatly.

Chief Kramer's eyes tightened. "Involved in what, Mr Smith?" He threw the gauntlet down, daring Albert to show his hand.

Undeterred Albert said, "In whatever is really going on at Unlimited Horizons, Chief Kramer. I haven't figured out what it is yet, but if you are not involved, you might want to distance yourself from Mayor Schultz. He isn't who you think he is ."

The chief of police gave himself a handful of seconds to consider Albert's stark warning, before leaning forward in his chair to respond.

His voice a growl, the town's senior police officer said, "Mr Smith, I understand you are here visiting old friends. I recommend you focus on enjoying that visit. Sightseeing. Reminiscing about old times. Not nocturnal adventures."

"Is that a threat, Chief Kramer?"

"A recommendation. From a current public servant to a former one." Kramer's smile was as warm as an Arctic winter. "You were a police officer once. You understand how these things work. Mayor Schultz is an important man in this town. He has many friends, many supporters. It would be unfortunate if your visit was cut short due to a misunderstanding."

Albert met Kramer's gaze without flinching. "I've never been very good at ignoring misunderstandings, Chief Kramer. Especially when they involve people getting hurt."

Kramer stood, straightening his uniform with a sharp tug. "Then perhaps you should consider who might get hurt if you continue down this path." His gaze unwavering, he said, "Your friends? The young woman? Your dog?"

Albert rose as well, the sofa creaking as he stood. "I'll keep that in mind. Thank you for the visit, Chief Kramer. It's been most illuminating."

Kramer offered his hand again. Albert shook it, feeling the increased pressure in the grip, the warning squeeze.

"Good day, Mr Smith. Enjoy the rest of your stay in Hoffenholen." Kramer turned to leave, then paused. "Oh, and if you should happen to see the intruders from last night, you might let them know that the mayor is quite distressed about his pet's injury. Quite distressed indeed."

With that, he strode to the door and left the hotel, his back ramrod straight, every inch the authority figure.

Albert watched him go before sinking back onto the sofa. The implications were clear. Kramer knew they had broken into the compound. He knew Rex had been injured by the panther. But he didn't have the evidence to secure a conviction. Whether he went looking for it or not he couldn't guess, but Albert suspected, yet again, that the mayor had a hand in the police chief's decision.

Arresting the famous Albert Smith, for that was what some people considered him to be, would draw attention where the mayor didn't want it. Likewise, killing him, if that was the sort of tactic Horst Schultz would employ, would spark an investigation he could not afford.

No, the mayor wanted this handled quietly. Albert pursed his lips and frowned.

Quietly? Was there a way to exploit the mayor's desires?

"Everything all right?"

The unexpected voice startled Albert and he snapped his head around so fast it almost travelled back in time.

Beverly was next to his elbow, a concerned expression on her face.

When his heart returned to a normal rhythm, he said, "Not exactly."

"What did he want?"

"To warn us off. In the politest way possible, of course."

Beverly sat beside him. "What did you tell him."

"That if he isn't involved, he should distance himself."

Beverly sighed. "What if he is involved, Albert?"

"Then we're in trouble."

Her eyes flaring, she said, "We were already in trouble."

Albert shrugged. "More trouble then."

Beverly sighed, shaking her head with a mixture of exasperation and resignation. "I think I'd better go wake Roy."

With Beverly headed upstairs, Albert continued to consider their situation. Kramer's visit had confirmed several things. First, they were definitely onto something significant. Second, his worry the mayor's influence extended into the local police force appeared to have substance to it. And third, they needed to be much more careful from now on.

The breakfast room was beginning to fill with other hotel guests. Albert watched them for a moment – normal people on normal holidays, completely unaware of the strange and potentially dangerous situation unfolding around them.

Albert smiled grimly. Things were moving forward. Chief Kramer had just made it abundantly clear how high the stakes were, but Albert had never been one to walk away from a mystery, especially when people's lives hung in the balance.

Rising from the sofa, he headed back to the breakfast room for another cup of coffee. It was going to be a long day.

Chapter 17

Taking a second cup of coffee with him, Albert retreated to the hotel's tiny courtyard garden to make a call before Roy and the others joined him for breakfast. The hotel's outside space was barely large enough to qualify as a garden - more of a horticultural afterthought with three potted plants, one of which appeared to be in the final stages of botanical surrender. Nevertheless, it offered some privacy, which was what Albert wanted.

He dialled Gary's number, watching a bee investigate one of the struggling plants with more enthusiasm than it deserved.

"Dad?" Gary answered on the second ring. "Are you okay?"

"I'm fine," Albert assured him, only then realising the time difference meant it was early in England and his call had most likely worried his eldest child. "My reason for calling is because I think I have uncovered something to do with Bitcoin, and I genuinely haven't the slightest clue what that even means."

"Bitcoin? I thought you were dealing with a woman who ran away from a cult?"

"I was. I am. That led to this." Albert wanted answers, not questions and thought he'd trained his kids better than that. When he held the rank of detective superintendent, Albert's subordinates were encouraged to ask questions, but only if they moved the investigation forward. Trying to clarify facts they already knew was a waste of everyone's time and he refused to tolerate it. Taking a deep breath and recognising that much of his impatience was to do with fatigue from lack of sleep, he said, "What can you tell me about Bitcoin crimes? Is that a thing?"

"I should say so, Dad. Not that I've ever had direct involvement in any, but I know of a few. Money laundering is the obvious one. Because Bitcoin transactions don't go through traditional banking systems, they're harder to track. Perfect for cleaning dirty money."

"Go on," Albert encouraged, watching as the determined bee gave up on the wilting plant and buzzed off to find more promising prospects elsewhere.

"Sorry, Dad, this isn't my area of expertise, but I can go speak to the forensic accountancy guys. They'll know all about it. Can I call you back when I know more?"

"Of course."

Gary wanted to make small talk, checking in on a father he considered too elderly to be galivanting across Europe all alone. Albert indulged him, playing down his rising sense of unease to make Hoffenholen sound like a peaceful paradise.

Spotting Roy and Beverly entering the restaurant, Albert waved through a window, failed to get their attention and made his excuses. Mila had just come in behind them, looking around nervously. They had Rex with them and Albert knew his dog would need to run around outside to relieve himself if nothing else.

Mila spotted Albert when he came in, nudging Beverly and pointing to bring her attention his way.

"Rex needs a walk," she said, closing the distance. "We all want breakfast, but his needs should come first."

"Ready for a walk, old boy?" Roy asked.

The question wasn't aimed at Rex, but he wagged his tail all the same. He was used to his human letting him out the moment he was awake, and his needs would become desperate soon.

Albert nodded. "Yes, that's a good idea. We need to talk, anyway." He was deliberate in not looking at Mila when he said it. Turning about, he led them back to the small garden and through it to reach the street outside.

No one said anything until they were fifty yards from the hotel, and it was Roy who spoke first.

"Beverly told us you've been chatting with the local constabulary."

"Chief of Police Gerhard Kramer," Albert confirmed, letting Rex off his lead so he could walk ahead and explore. "Charming fellow. Thinks the world of Mayor Schultz."

"What did he say?" Mila asked, her eyes wide with worry.

"He delivered a friendly warning. He knows it was me who broke into Unlimited Horizons last night and suggested that I mind my own business." Albert turned his gaze directly to Mila. "He also mentioned something interesting about you."

Mila tensed visibly. "What did he say?"

"He said you were caught breaking into a restricted area of the camp before you escaped." Albert kept his tone neutral, not accusatory, but direct. "You didn't mention that part."

Everyone focused their attention on the youngest member of the team.

Mila looked embarrassed, but said, "I told you there were rooms under the ground. How else do you think I knew about them?"

Albert asked, "What happened."

"I was desperate to find Talia and they wouldn't let me even confirm she was there. I was supposed to just take their word for it. After eight weeks of their excuses, I decided to look for her myself."

"Go on," Albert encouraged when she hesitated.

"There are doors that only staff can go through. I told you this already. They have electronic locks operated by those badges they wear." Mila's voice grew more confident as she continued. "I saw Sabrina use hers one day. She was distracted, talking to someone, and it was on her coat when she took it off and left it on a desk. I grabbed it when no one was looking."

"You stole her security badge?" Roy questioned.

Mila shrugged. "I was going to put it back. I just wanted to find Talia."

"And did you?" Beverly asked.

Mila shook her head. "I only got through two doors before I was caught. The first one led to a corridor with more doors. The second opened into a stairwell. I was at the bottom of the stairs when two guards found me."

Albert leaned forward. "Going down? Into the underground bunkers Roy talked about?"

"I guess so," Mila said. "I didn't know there were bunkers then. Talia had to be somewhere, and I was only at the camp to find her." Her expression darkened. "They weren't gentle when they caught me. They took the badge, dragged me back to my room, and locked me in for two days with only water and bread. After that, they watched me constantly. That's when I decided I had to escape."

"Did you see anything else?" Albert asked. "Anything unusual?"

Mila considered the question. "Not really. Although …" she chewed on her bottom lip, deep in thought for a few moments. "I passed a server room. It was a big one. I used to work for an architectural firm, and they had more than a hundred employees all on their computers at the same time. This server room was bigger than the one they had."

"And this was underground?" Albert tried to clarify.

"Yes." Mila nodded. "It was inside the restricted area. The only way to access it is with one of those security badges I told you about. Only the staff have them."

"Which means," Albert said, thinking out loud, "that whatever's happening in those underground areas isn't part of their spiritual journey."

"Maybe that's the real operation," Roy concluded, "and the cult is just a cover."

"I've been giving this some thought. The identity thing is bugging me." Albert added. "People surrender everything, including who they are. It wouldn't take much to put those identities to work."

Beverly, who had been quiet until now, asked, "Do you think Talia is actually there? Or could they have been lying about that too?"

The question hung in the air, heavy with implication. Mila's face drained of colour.

"She has to be there," she whispered. "She has to be."

Albert wished he could offer reassurance, but the truth was he didn't know. If Unlimited Horizons was as corrupt as he suspected, there was no telling what might have happened to Talia.

"We'll find her," Albert promised. "But to do that, we need to understand exactly what we're dealing with."

"What did your son tell you about the Bitcoin?" Roy asked, steering the conversation back to practicalities.

"He told me Bitcoin crime is a real thing but wanted to consult some of his colleagues before telling me more. It's not his area of expertise," he explained. "We need to look into Unlimited Horizons, find out if anyone else has escaped or reported concerns. And we need to know more about Sabrina Aldridge. Mila, you said her online profile looked fake?"

Mila nodded. "Identical posts across multiple platforms. No real interaction, just broadcasting."

"Then that's where we start," Albert decided.

Roy clapped him on the shoulder. "Righto, old boy. You tell us what to do and we'll do our best to help. This is your show."

Albert clapped his hands together and called to turn Rex around. "First things first. I need some breakfast."

Chapter 18

Forty-five minutes later, their bellies filled, the team were back in Mila's room. Beverly's laptop sat open on the desk, surrounded by notepads covered with scribbled observations. Roy's phone was propped against a water glass, displaying an article about cryptocurrency fraud. Mila was curled in the armchair with a tablet scrutinizing social media profiles.

Albert, meanwhile, paced back and forth across the carpet.

Confused about what the humans were doing, or even talking about, Rex had found a quiet corner and was happily snoozing. There were many human concepts Rex couldn't grasp, and money was one of them. He saw his human hand over pieces of paper or coins, or more frequently now, tap his card on a machine to make it beep before he took the goods he wanted. Except when they went to a pub or restaurant where he ate first and then did the beeping thing. It was all quite bizarre.

"Nothing," Mila announced, dropping the tablet onto her lap in frustration. "I've looked through every social media platform I can think of. There's not a single mention of anyone who's been at Unlimited Horizons apart from the official accounts. No reviews, no personal stories, nothing."

"That's odd, isn't it?" Beverly remarked, looking up from her laptop. "People post about everything these days. Holidays, restaurant meals, the colour of their socks. But not a word about a life-changing spiritual retreat?"

"It's more than odd," Albert said, pausing his pacing. "It's deliberate. Think about it - they take people's devices, cut them off from the outside world. If anyone leaves, they're probably made to sign non-disclosure agreements."

"Or they don't leave at all," Roy muttered darkly.

A heavy silence followed his words. None of them wanted to consider that possibility, but it couldn't be ignored.

"Look at this," Beverly said, breaking the uncomfortable quiet. She turned her laptop around to show them the screen. "I've been searching for any businesses connected to Unlimited Horizons or Mayor Schultz. There's nothing official, but I found this."

The screen displayed a sleek, professional-looking website for something called 'Digital Ascension Investments'. The logo featured a stylized human figure transforming into a series of binary digits - zeros and ones flowing upward like a digital spirit leaving its earthly body.

"This is what I found when I typed in 'Digital Ascension'. I don't know that it's the same people or even anything to do with them, but it strikes me as something of a coincidence if it isn't them."

"Transform your financial future," Albert read from the headline. "Our team of expert advisors will help you ascend beyond traditional investment limitations."

"Scroll down," Beverly instructed.

Albert used the touchpad to navigate down the page. There were testimonials from satisfied clients, each accompanied by a professional headshot and impressive credentials. He read some aloud, "Dr. Klaus Weber, Financial Analyst with twenty years of experience in market prediction. Anna Becker, Investment Strategist, former advisor to European banking institutions."

Beverly took the laptop back and clicked on another page. "They're promoting a revolutionary cryptocurrency investment system. Guaranteed returns of thirty percent annually. Exclusive access for select clients."

Roy grabbed his phone. "I've just been reading something like that." Everyone waited while he scrolled to find the right page. "Yes, here it is. Now, I don't know if I've got this right, but what you just described, my love, sounds just like something they call a Ponzi scheme. Apparently, they make it look real by using the money they get from new investors to pay out to the earlier ones. It creates the illusion of legitimate profits."

Albert was already concerned about identity theft. How that could be used in conjunction with this he didn't know. His phone started to ring, the screen displaying the name 'Gary' once again. He snatched it up, talking almost before the call had a chance to connect.

"Hey, son, have you got something for me?"

"Hello, Dad. I have you on speaker phone. I'm with the computer fraud guys. I'm going to let them explain."

A second voice came on the phone, this one that of a younger woman.

"Hello, Mr Smith."

"Albert, please. You're on speaker phone at this end too. I have some of my friends with me."

"Okay, Albert, I'm Melanie. Superintendent Smith tells me you might have stumbled across a Bitcoin scam?"

"Well, maybe. To be honest, I don't really know what that would look like. Hence the call to my son. If this is an illegal operation intended to defraud people out of their money, then it's taking place inside a secure community and might also involve identity theft. I'm guessing the last part, though. That could be a total red herring."

Melanie didn't reply straight away, the folks in the hotel room in Germany treated to the sound of a muted discussion at the other end.

When Melanie's voice returned a few moments later, she said, "We're going to need a little more time to look into this, Albert. I have the name of the company, Unlimited Horizons, from Superintendent Smith already."

Interrupting quickly, Albert said, "Wait, do you think this is a real scam then?"

"I don't know enough to make a call on that yet. We are going to investigate, though."

Albert knew he was talking to people in the Metropolitan Police in London. They had no jurisdiction in Germany, but a single phone call would link them to Interpol or Europol … there were people and organisations they could mobilise. But …

"I'm the guy on the ground," he said. "What can I do that will help? What information do you need?"

Gary responded instantly. "Dad, you're seventy-eight. What you should do right now is pack your things and go to your next destination."

Reminding him of his age was the absolutely best strategy to employ if he wanted Albert to dig his heels in. He could have protested about his son's ageism, but instead Albert laughed and said, "And you think I won't get into just as much trouble when I arrive there? Melanie, dear, why don't you tell me how I can help?"

Albert could imagine his son glaring at the younger woman who was undoubtedly many ranks lower. But she worked in a different department and had her own boss, a fact that became quite apparent when another new voice came on the phone.

"Mr Smith, this is Superintendent Derek Hope. I run the computer fraud division. I must apologise for eavesdropping on your conversation, but what you report is of great interest to me. These kinds of schemes, if that is what you have uncovered, are incredibly hard to prove and the culprits get away all too often. Usually taking millions of other peoples' hard-earned money with them. If you are in a position to help, I am not above asking you to do so."

They all heard Gary growl, "Derek. A word."

The line went quiet, telling Albert and the others the two senior police officers had removed themselves to 'discuss' the matter in private.

"Are you still there, Melanie?" Albert asked.

"I'm here."

"Super. I still don't really understand how any of this works. Why don't you give it to me at the most basic level? How do con artists make money with cryptocurrency?"

"Right, okay." She said it like she was cracking her fingers to warm up. "To start with, criminal enterprises use Bitcoin to launder money."

"Yes, that's what Gary told me. I get how that could work. What else?"

"Then there's fraud - setting up fake investment schemes, promising huge returns, collecting real money in exchange for worthless digital tokens. The anonymity of cryptocurrency makes it easier to disappear with the cash."

Albert thought again about the list of names they'd found, the professions noted beside them. "What if someone were using stolen identities for these schemes?"

A pause. "That would be sophisticated," Melanie said slowly. "They could set up investment platforms using the stolen identities. They could show what appear to be real people investing their money and so create trust to bring in real investors. Or they could even, and I'm spit balling here, make it look like the people behind it are the ones whose identities they stole. When the scheme collapses, the real people whose identities were stolen would take the blame."

"And how much money could be involved?"

"Millions, easily. Bitcoin's value fluctuates wildly, but a single Bitcoin is worth tens of thousands of euros right now."

Albert rubbed his chin thoughtfully. "We found a note that mentioned an extraction. What might that mean?"

"Moving the money out of the cryptocurrency ecosystem and into traditional financial systems, probably through a series of complex transactions to hide the trail. Classic money laundering."

Albert nodded; the pieces were starting to fit together in his mind. "One more thing - what kind of setup would you need for something like this? Could you run it from a laptop in a hotel room?"

Melanie laughed. "No way. You'd need serious computing power, especially if you're running multiple fake accounts and moving large sums. Plus high-speed internet connections, backup systems, security protocols … It would be a proper operation."

"Like one you might hide in an underground bunker, for instance?"

"Exactly like that," Melanie agreed, then paused. "Albert, have you seen something like that where you are?"

"No," Albert looked at Mila. "But we are with someone who has. You said you need to know more. Would it help if I sent you some pictures?"

Beverly's eyes almost popped out. "What? Albert you can't seriously be thinking about going back there! You were almost caught last night. Rex got injured, my husband almost had a heart attack from the exertion …"

"Steady now, old girl," Roy protested.

Ignoring him, she pressed on, "And the chief of police is already onto you. What do you think he will do if you ignore his warning and sneak back in there?"

Albert grinned wolfishly. "Who said anything about sneaking? I'm going to walk through the front door."

Roy snorted a laugh he tried hard to suppress and had to look away when his wife scowled at him.

Over the phone, Melanie warned. "Be careful, Albert. Cryptocurrency crimes are big money and the people behind them are ruthless. If that's what this is, there's no telling what they might do to protect themselves if they feel exposed."

Gary's voice came back on the line. "Dad, I don't want you getting involved. Despite your track record, the right thing to do is walk away."

"Too late for that," Albert replied. "The police chief already paid me a visit this morning."

"Dad!" The exasperation in Gary's voice was palpable. "This isn't your fight. Stand back and let the professionals take over."

"They can't do that unless they know there is a crime to investigate, son. You forget, Gary, that I know how police business works and that the bigger the crime and the more agencies there are involved, the more bureaucratic it becomes."

"So you're planning to confront a cult leader who may also be running a massive cryptocurrency fraud?"

Albert's voice came out dripping with innocence. "I wouldn't dream of it."

"You're a terrible liar, Dad."

"So your mother always said. I'll call you back when I know more."

Ending the call before his son could waste yet more time and energy trying to talk him out of it, Albert looked around the room. No one said anything, but everyone looked his way. Even Rex had his head off the carpet, anticipating what might come next.

It was a tense moment. The chases through the woods, both Mila's yesterday, and then the one Roy, Rex, and Albert endured a few hours ago drove home how precarious their situation could be. There had been no violence so far, unless one counted Rex's fight with the panther, but the mayor and his people knew where Albert and his friends were staying.

A knock at the door cut through the room like a thunderclap, the effect not too dissimilar from throwing a grenade through the window. Hearts stopped, Rex barked, and all eyes turned to stare at the room's only exit.

Chapter 19

Her heart in her mouth, Beverly called out, "Who is it?"

The heavily accented voice of a young woman echoed back through the door. "Housekeeping."

Beverly rolled her eyes and started for the door only to find Roy's arm blocking her path.

"What if that's a bluff?" he hissed so the people in the room would hear but the maid (if it really was housekeeping outside) wouldn't. "It could be an assassin."

Mila swallowed hard, but Albert crossed the room to peek through the spyhole. He opened the door a moment later to reveal a portly middle-aged woman with a housekeeping cart laden with cleaning products and fresh towels.

"Can you return later?" he asked with a smile. "Sorry, we need the room at the moment."

Showing how little she cared, the maid nodded and moved to the opposite side of the corridor to knock there instead.

Albert closed the door and turned around, leaning his back against it. The unexpected knock had made him jump too. They were skittish and it demonstrated what he already knew: this wasn't something Beverly and Roy ought to be mixed up in. Mila had a personal stake in the outcome, and he was … well, Albert knew he had a tenacious nature that didn't like to see a mystery go unsolved or an injustice unpunished. He could, in fact, on occasion, get a little Old Testament about such things. Not that he proposed to rain fire and brimstone upon Mayor Schultz and his people, but if they were defrauding people and ruining lives, he just couldn't walk away.

He licked his lips, pushed away from the door, and started to articulate his thoughts.

"Listen, guys, I think my son is right. This isn't something we should be mixed up in."

"Thank goodness," said Beverly. "Finally, some sense."

Mila said nothing, but the disappointment was there on her face for Albert to see.

"I'm going to stay to help Mila find her sister, but I think the two of you should move onto wherever you planned to go next."

"And leave you, old boy? I think not." Roy's response was as Albert expected.

"But, darling ..." Beverly rose to her feet.

Roy pulled her into a hug. "I'm sorry, kitten. I'm the man you married. I've flown fighter jets down the enemy's throat and clipped the waves of hurricane seas in an ailing aircraft while trying to land on the heaving deck of an aircraft carrier. Walking away when a friend needs my help isn't something I can do."

"All the same," Albert knew he was going to have a fight to get them to leave, "I will be able to move more freely if I don't have to worry about the two of you."

"And all the while we'll be worrying about you," Roy argued. "Forget it, old boy. We're staying to see this thing through. Now, when you were talking to Melanie, you said you were going to walk right up to the gates and into the Unlimited Horizons camp. Why don't you tell us how you are going to pull that off."

Mila had a single tear running from her right eye. She swiped at it when she saw Albert notice and smiled in an embarrassed way.

Albert nodded to himself and said, "Okay. Here's what I propose."

Chapter 20

When Albert finished speaking, his audience stared at him in stark disbelief. His plan was simple, and it was genius. It required a little setting up, but that would take hours rather than days and could be put into motion immediately.

With that in mind, Beverly and Mila squeezed in next to each other with the laptop at their hands, and Albert made sure his phone was charged – it was about to take a battering.

An hour later, his jaw ached from talking and the strip of carpet he'd paced needed a break. But his idea had worked better than even Albert hoped it could and now they had some time to kill.

"You should change," said Mila.

Albert looked down at his clothes. "What's wrong with what I'm wearing?"

"Nothing," Mila said carefully. "Buuuuut …"

"She's right," said Beverly, getting to her feet. "You unpacked your clothes yesterday, didn't you?"

"Um, yeah." Albert watched Roy's wife cross to the built-in wardrobe where she rifled through his meagre selection of outfits.

She pulled out his favourite navy-blue jacket. "This one. And you should wear it with a white shirt."

Roy said, "You'll need a tie, old boy."

"I've got one." Albert squeezed around Beverly to reach into the wardrobe, draping it across his right arm to show them when he turned around.

"Oh, that won't do at all, old boy," said Roy, his eyes wide as though recoiling in horror.

Albert looked at it. "What's wrong with it?"

"Well," said Beverly. "For a start it's got a tear in it."

"That's just a little age. Gives it character, don't you think?"

"Secondly," Beverly continued. "It's hideous. The best thing for this," Beverly gently lifted the tie from Albert's arm and began to fold it neatly, "is to give it the burial it deserves."

Albert frowned with dismay when she dropped it into the bin.

"Roy," she clicked her fingers. "Tie selection if you please."

Roy bustled away with a, "Right you are, my love," returning from their room next door a few moments later with a half dozen ties on a clever hanger designed for precisely that purpose.

Albert knew Roy always wore a tie unless the temperature rose too high – not that common in England, so he shouldn't have been surprised to see the display.

"This one," Beverly selected a tie that was bold burgundy and navy-blue diagonal stripes. Holding it against the jacket, she nodded approvingly. "Yes?"

Albert wasn't sure it was any better at all, but doubted arguing was worth the effort. He would rescue his old tie later when there was no one around.

"Okay, so I have an outfit you approve of. What about Mila?"

The subject of Mila's outfit proved simpler. They wanted Albert to look smart, but Mila was supposed to look almost homeless and that was going to be easy to achieve.

Albert checked his watch: they had more than two hours to kill and all that needed to happen between now and when they left the hotel was a dog walk for Rex and a light lunch.

A call to reception confirmed they could book a table in the restaurant to take care of the latter and Rex was sound asleep so the former could wait.

"So what shall we do now?" asked Mila. "Do we keep digging?"

"Yes," said Albert. "Let's keep digging."

For the next hour, they scoured the internet for anything related to Unlimited Horizons, Mayor Schultz, or the Bitcoin platform. About the mayor they found a wealth of information. There were photographs and interviews, newspaper reports, and more, but Unlimited Horizons barely appeared at all. All they turned up was the website which promised spiritual healing and digital ascension (that phrase again) to anyone who wanted to escape the twenty-first century trappings.

They searched for but could not find a link between the website Digital Ascensions Investments firm Beverly found and the Unlimited Horizons Spiritual Retreat. They did, however, find a list of the board members along with photographs.

Albert asked, "Can you print the names?"

Beverly offered him a one eyebrow raised look. "Not without a printer."

"Good point." Albert collected his notepad and wrote them down, just the way he would have done back in his days on the force.

"If this *is* them, I wonder if the list of names will match up to any real people."

Motivated by Albert's question, Mila took the first name on the list and typed it into a new search. "Let's see if we can find them." She got a hit with the first name. "Franko Rosso sounds Italian, but there's no social media profile for him whatsoever. There should be something, even if it's a work history."

"You mean like Linked-In?" Beverly asked.

Albert held up his hand. "Linked what?"

Mila explained how many professionals have a presence on a platform called *Linked-In*. There they would do online business and could be found and contacted. Apparently, it was good for job hunting and networking.

"I think the letters after his name mean he's a lawyer." She pointed to the screen on the Digital Ascensions Investments website. "I ought to be able to find something about him."

Albert scratched his chin. "In the UK, directors of businesses have to be registered on Companies House. There is literally no way to have no online presence."

Roy spoke the conclusion they were all thinking. "He's been scrubbed."

"You mean digitally ascended," said Mila, taking the name of the next director and performing the same checks.

No one voiced surprise when she got the same result. She tried again and again, checking enough of the firm's listed board members to be certain there was no fluke.

"Stolen identities," Albert murmured. "The names are probably real. The faces might be too, but I think we will discover Franko Rosso and the rest of the board are living inside Unlimited Horizons. He thought for a second. "Mila, can you bring up what you found for Sabrina again, please?" Something bothered him about Sabrina Aldridge's role and her supposed fake profile. As Horst's right-hand woman, she had to be deeply involved.

"Sure. What do you want to know?"

"What are you thinking?" Roy asked.

"I'm thinking that Horst may be the public face of this operation, but Sabrina strikes me as the brains," Albert replied. "If we can figure out who she really is, we might find a crack in their facade."

For the next half hour, they worked in focused silence, broken only by the occasional tap of keys or muttered observation. Rex returned to his nap, his legs twitching occasionally as he dream-chased squirrels.

"Albert," Mila finally said, her voice tense with excitement. "I think I've found something."

They gathered around the tablet, where Mila had pulled up a series of photographs from Sabrina's various social media accounts. She had arranged them chronologically, going back several years.

"Look at these pictures from four years ago," she said, pointing to images of Sabrina at various locations around Europe. "The captions mention her working in finance in Zurich."

"So?" Roy asked, not seeing the significance.

"So look at this one," Mila swiped to a photo of Sabrina supposedly taken in front of the Zurich Opera House in August 2021. "The Opera House was covered in scaffolding for renovations from March 2021 to January 2022. It couldn't have looked like this."

Albert's eyes narrowed. "She's faking her timeline."

"Exactly. And there's more." Mila swiped through several more photos, pointing out inconsistencies in the backgrounds, impossible weather conditions for the stated dates, even a restaurant that had closed two years before she claimed to have dined there.

"She's created a fake history," Beverly said slowly. "But why go to all that trouble?"

"Because she's not really Sabrina Aldridge," Albert concluded. "She's someone else entirely." When Mila first suggested Sabrina's profile might be fake, he couldn't understand why someone would go to the trouble. Now it seemed obvious.

"Then we need to find out who she really is," said Roy.

Albert pulled out his phone. "I'm sending these pictures to Gary. He might be able to identify her."

He selected several of the clearest images of Sabrina and sent them to his son with a brief explanation of what they suspected. Gary's reply came back almost immediately: "On it. Give me a few hours."

"Now what?" Beverly asked when Albert reported that Gary was looking into it.

"Now we all take Rex for a short walk – there's safety in numbers. And then we get some lunch. This afternoon is going to be busy."

Chapter 21

The sky was thick with rain clouds when Beverly's BMW pulled up to the gates of Unlimited Horizons. Albert straightened his borrowed tie, his outfit doing its job and making him look more like a retired banker than a meddling pensioner with a habit of stumbling into trouble. The formal attire was deliberate – an attempt to project authority and respectability.

"Looks like they're all here," Roy remarked from the back seat, peering through the window at the cluster of vehicles already parked on the road to either side of the compound's imposing fence.

Albert nodded with satisfaction. His phone calls had struck a chord with the media. Using his name to attract their attention was an alien concept that felt not only ugly, but abusive. He wasn't going to give them the spectacle they expected. They were here for a big story, and he doubted very much he was going to be able to pull that off. Rather, he was using them to force the mayor's hand. Mila had been kept from her sister, but would they be able to continue that policy with the world's press watching? He didn't think so.

And that was the point. Mila asked for his help to rescue Talia and that was what he planned to do. Taking down the Bitcoin operation and the whole identity theft thing was a bigger challenge than he wanted to face. Not that he even knew for sure if it was happening. The clues he had would be inadmissible and it was possible he was misinterpreting them. Regardless, Albert wondered if maybe Gary was right to worry this time.

If they could find and reclaim Talia, Albert would consider it a victory.

By the time Albert opened his door, reporters were swarming his way.

"Are you sure about this?" Beverly asked, her hands still gripping the steering wheel even though they'd stopped. "It feels like we're walking straight into the lion's den."

"Lions," Albert replied, "are generally more cautious when observed by an audience."

Rex, squeezed into the back seat with Roy and Mila, gave a soft woof of agreement. Despite his injuries, the dog seemed eager for another adventure.

Mila leaned forward between the front seats. Her hair was tidy but a long way from salon perfect and the outfit she picked from those Beverly purchased, was one that didn't really fit. The effect was exactly as intended – she looked like someone who had been through an ordeal.

"What if they still won't let me see her?" she voiced that which concerned her most.

Albert had no answer, but said, "We'll cross that bridge when we come to it."

With that thought in their minds, they exited the car. The moment they stepped out, microphones appeared under Albert's nose and cameras swung between him and Mila.

"Is this the woman you told us about, Albert?" more than one journalist asked. The question came in a multitude of accents including good old BBC English.

Albert locked onto the team from England – his natural inclination was to deal with them in favour of anyone else simply because they spoke the same language, but he was in Germany …

Singling out a news firm he knew, Albert extended his hand. "Thank you for coming."

"Mr. Smith," the reporter had a firm grasp. "Dieter Reimann, Deutsche Welle. Thank you for contacting us." His English was impeccable, his handshake firm. "These are my colleagues from ARD and ZDF." He indicated two other men and a woman with bright red hair who were hurrying to join them.

Albert shook hands all around. "This is Mila Petrov," he introduced her, "whose sister Talia has been kept from her at Unlimited Horizons for months. And these are my friends, Roy and Beverly Hope."

"Is your information solid, Mr. Smith?" Dieter asked, his expression serious.

"It's solid," Albert confirmed. "This young woman has been systematically prevented from seeing her sister. Talia came here five months ago. All Mila wants is to confirm her sister is safe and well. She stayed inside the community for two months but was prevented from seeing her. They have segregated areas for residents at different points in their journey, and when Mila attempted to find Talia, she was kept in solitary isolation for two days. It may be the case that Talia is alive and well, but if that is true, she should be permitted to confirm it to her only living relative. In her bid to find Talia, Mila was forced to join the community and surrender all her identification including her bank cards. We discovered yesterday that Mila's bank account has been emptied while she was held captive inside this compound." To accentuate his point, Albert aimed a stiff arm at the gates where two armed guards stood looking confused and embarrassed about all the attention.

The information was a public retelling of the story he gave them over the phone just a few hours earlier. This time it was for the cameras.

The journalists exchanged glances. It was a compelling human-interest story. The sister seeking reunion, the mysterious spiritual retreat, the foreign visitor denied access – it had all the elements of a riveting news segment.

"Let's go, then," Dieter said, gesturing toward the gate.

As they approached, the uniformed guards watched warily from the security booth. They straightened as the group drew near, hands well away from their sidearms.

"Good afternoon," Dieter called out in German. "We're here for an interview regarding Unlimited Horizons and the Petrov sisters."

One of the guards stepped forward, his expression about as welcoming as a tax audit on Christmas morning. "No appointments today. The compound is closed to visitors." His eyes flicked to take in Mila, and it was obvious he recognised her.

"This isn't a visit," Dieter replied, switching to English for the benefit of Albert and the others. "We're here to cover a story of significant public interest."

The guard's face remained impassive. "No cameras allowed inside the compound. It violates our community's privacy policies."

"Are you holding Talia Petrov prisoner?" Dieter pressed. "How many other prisoners do you have?"

With all the cameras in his face and questions he didn't know how to answer, the guard didn't know what he was supposed to do. He wanted to repeat his message about the compound being closed to visitors, but Albert could see in his eyes that he knew that wasn't going to work.

Behind the front row of reporters, others were facing away from the camp, their cameramen capturing the interior behind them as they reported.

More of the journalists had questions and as the din grew, the guard backed away. Albert allowed himself a little smile when he saw him jabbering into his radio.

Less than a minute later, he saw Thomas and Bruno appear from the headquarters building. He'd taken them to be thugs and little more, but they clearly had a higher standing than he realised.

Thomas stormed toward the gate, leaving Bruno watching, his muscular arms folded over his chest. He saw Albert and then Mila, his expression darkening each time. He wasn't happy, and that pleased Albert no end.

Behind him the headquarters building looked different in the daylight. He'd seen it like that before, of course, but returning last night his memory of it was as a darkened mass of corridors and offices, a shadowy prison from which he and Roy had only barely escaped.

Thomas barked something at the guard, making the man bow his head and stare at the ground. The camera continued to roll, and they waited impatiently while Thomas sent the guard back to the gate.

He approached but didn't come close enough for convenient conversation. Rather, he hung back, sticking with his colleague so the reporters were forced to shout their questions. The guards acted as though they couldn't hear or understand, their eyes focussed impassively at the crowd of journalists baying to enter the camp.

Thomas spoke on his phone and Albert could guess who he was speaking to.

Chapter 22

Horst Schultz was enjoying the front nine of his favourite golf course in Gleichenkirchen, fifty miles to the south of Hoffenholen when the call came through. He didn't answer it, he had Sabrina for that, but shanked his shot into the rough to the right of the sixth fairway when he heard her swear.

"Bad luck," said Harold Bruner, the German Minister for Finance, not meaning it one bit. He was two shots down already and had a fat wager on being able to beat the small-town mayor. They'd gone to university in Berlin together more than thirty years earlier, both studying politics and finance. If asked, Harold would claim to have done better if their careers were to be compared side by side, but Horst didn't seem to be under the pressure Harold felt, his personal assistant was so gorgeous Harold struggled to concentrate on his game, and he was clearly making more money too. Worse yet, Horst was thinking about where his political career would go and Harold thought his old friend was capable of anything.

The move from small-town mayor to international politics isn't a simple one, but it had been done before. He was too charismatic, that was the problem. People did what Horst Schultz told them, rarely questioning whether they should until long after he'd achieved whatever it was he wanted from them.

Something, however, was currently amiss.

Harold lined up to take his tee shot but strained his hearing and took his time.

"What do you mean they are demanding to be allowed access?" Sabrina snapped. "Your task is to keep people out."

"But it's the BBC!" Thomas protested. "And RTL, and about seven other channels. The only ones not here are CNN! They are outside with their cameras with that old man and his dog and they are filming."

His head pressed in next to Sabrina's so he could hear too, Horst narrowed his eyes. "They are filming?"

He glanced over his shoulder, catching Harold clearly trying to hear what was being said. Taking Sabrina with him, he moved farther away.

"Have they made any other demands?" he asked.

Sounding distinctly put upon, Thomas whined, "Yes. It's that troublemaker, Mila. She wants to see her sister. I said we should have killed her when she broke into the bunker. She must have seen things, Horst."

"That's not for you to worry about, Thomas," Horst replied in his annoyingly calm manner. He wanted to tell Thomas how disappointingly one dimensional he was. This was an opportunity if viewed correctly. "This is what I want you to do …"

When the conversation ended a few moments later, Harold centred himself and took his shot. It sailed down the middle of the fairway, bouncing and skipping when it finally came back to earth. It was a peach of a shot, and with Horst in the rough he was going to reclaim at least one of his strokes, if not both.

"I'm sorry, Harold," Horst crossed the tee, his hand out for it to be shaken. "I'm afraid a situation has developed in Hoffenholen, and I am forced to return there. Local politics. I'm sure you understand."

"And our game?" Harold wasn't happy to be denied the chance to win.

"Let's call it a draw. I'm two shots ahead but you appear to have the better of me on this hole. We can keep the wager as it is and replay in the near future."

Harold considered arguing. He was happy to continue and wondered if he could push Horst to forfeit. Choosing to let it go, mostly because he knew Horst would laugh and question his desperate need to win if he pushed it, Harold shook his old friend's hand and thanked him for the game.

Walking back to the clubhouse and the carpark beyond, Horst dropped his smile.

"Albert Smith is beginning to really irritate me."

Sabrina expressed her surprise. "Then why did you let him into the camp, Horst? It's private property. We have every right to deny them access."

"Because not doing so makes us look like we have something to hide. If they interview our residents, what will they discover?"

Sabrina nodded, annoyed she hadn't thought of it from that angle. "They will find people who are happy and who have nothing but positive things to say about the Unlimited Horizons community."

"Precisely. Mila's sister is one of them."

"You think it wise to let them meet?"

Horst shrugged. "I think it doesn't matter. We haven't yet used Talia's identity for anything. If she wants to leave with her sister, she can go. If that happens in front of the cameras, we can make a big show out of how well she has done in our care. Think about how many new applicants we will have."

"Our *sponsor*," she chose the word carefully, "will not like the exposure."

"Perhaps not, but you can leave that for me to handle. If he calls, I will reassure him. Everything we do for him depends on the success of Unlimited Horizons. That is the cover that hides our operation. Besides, you said it yourself when we first set this up: A hustler has to get out of town as quick as he can, but a good conman, well he doesn't have to leave until he wants to. Neither the cameras nor Albert Smith will glimpse more than a shadow of what we have really been doing for the past five years."

"And if Albert Smith knows more than you think?"

"Then I will kill him myself."

"You know, you probably won't have a choice. When our sponsor learns about this, he'll expect to hear you have already dealt with it."

Showing the first traces of irritation; he really didn't need to be reminded who they were working with, Horst said, "Thank you, Sabrina. Perhaps when he calls, I will tell him it was your fault."

Sabrina's lips twitched, but she bit down her retort.

They hurried to their car where the driver was surprised to see them back so soon. Mayor Schultz wanted to return to Hoffenholen and there was no mistaking the sense of urgency.

Chapter 23

Ten minutes had passed since they arrived outside the gates to the Unlimited Horizons compound. The clouds continued to gather, and the first distant rumble of thunder rolled across the sky like a cosmic bowling ball.

Turning to Dieter, Albert asked, "What happens if they continue to deny us access?"

Dieter opened his mouth to reply, but at that moment, Thomas ended his call and summoned the guards. A short one-sided conversation ensued, ending with the guards jogging back to the gate.

"You can enter," one announced. He waved to the second guard inside the booth and the barrier – little more than a steel pole – swung upward to allow them through. The guard initially objected to Rex's presence, but Albert merely raised an eyebrow and waited. After a moment of mutual staring, the guard relented with a disgruntled shrug.

In daylight, with no panther chasing him, Albert had a better opportunity to observe the place. On his first visit, he'd been too caught off guard to look about, but it looked remarkably normal—clean, orderly, almost like a small college campus. But he knew better than most how appearances could deceive.

As they walked along the immaculate driveway, Albert noticed people emerging from the accommodation buildings ahead. They wore simple, earth-toned clothing and expressions of mild curiosity. Some carried books or gardening tools, suggesting they'd been interrupted in the middle of their daily activities.

"Where are they?" Mila murmured. "I don't see Horst or Sabrina."

Albert had noticed the same. The mayor's absence was especially conspicuous. A man who clearly enjoyed the spotlight would normally leap at the chance to show off his spiritual community to the press. His absence suggested either he hadn't been informed, which felt unlikely, or he was deliberately staying away.

Meanwhile Thomas, who had fixed his face and was now smiling like a gameshow contestant, came forward with his arms open.

"On behalf of the facilitator here at Unlimited Horizons, I am instructed to welcome you all to move freely. Please record whatever you wish. Please speak to whomever you choose, but please also respect the privacy of our residents. Many are here because they wished to escape the outside world. Some have had to overcome addiction issues or are actively trying to. Their recovery and long-term health is our greatest concern, not your desire to ensure everything here is above board. We have nothing to hide, but there are areas of our operation to which you will not have access."

"Why is that?" asked Dieter, a microphone in his hand and a cameraman making sure to capture Thomas' response.

Thomas smiled benevolently. "As I already explained, the long-term health of our residents is our greatest concern. They want privacy and it is our job to provide that for them. They surrender their identities upon joining us. It is part of a process our leader calls digital ascension. We cleanse them of the digital filth that fills their lives, freeing them to be more spiritually whole. The restricted areas are where we store and manage their identities."

They were walking slowly up the main road leading through the former RAF airbase. The headquarters building loomed to their front but Thomas steered them away from it.

"What of Mila Petrov's bank accounts?" Dieter asked. "They were emptied while she was a resident here. Once she surrendered all her bank cards, only Unlimited Horizon's had access to her funds."

With the microphone thrust back under his nose, Thomas almost laughed.

"This is a retreat for people who need help. Mila surrendered her bank accounts, both checking and savings, when she entered the facility. This was explained when she first came to us."

"No, it wasn't!" Mila snapped.

Thomas looked her way for the first time. "Mila, we have your signature on the forms you signed. You legally surrendered everything you had so we could look after it until such time as you considered yourself ready to leave." He looked into the camera again. "It is our great hope that all our residents will one day leave, but we don't press any of them to do so. We cannot operate without cashflow – the residents must be fed and housed and looked after while they are here. We have medical professionals on the staff, gardeners …" he indicated the grounds. "The funds we take are invested by some very clever people, the profit made is used to operate this facility."

Mila had heard enough. Albert asked that she stay quiet when they entered the camp, but her patience was at an end.

"You locked me in a cell!" she spat.

"We detained you and separated you from the other residents when you broke what is pretty much the only rule we have. Honestly, Mila, it's never happened before, and we really didn't know what to do with you. I think we all regret the event, but for all we knew, you were trying to access the private information of our residents; vulnerable people who require and deserve our protection. You gave us no choice. We had to keep you away from everyone else until we could figure out how to manage you."

"That's nothing but lies, Thomas. I was trying to get to my sister, and you know it."

Dieter interrupted the exchange. "I believe Mila was chased through the woods when she tried to escape."

"I was."

"That flies in the face of your claim to let people leave when they feel they are ready."

Thomas nodded. "It would, but Mila is framing the incident to make us look like the bad guys. She ran and two of our guard dogs – employed to patrol the perimeter to keep intruders out - gave chase. We were worried about her frame of mind and how the dogs might react when they caught up to her. Mila showed aggression many times while she was with us and we were concerned she might hurt the dogs or that in turn they might hurt her as they defended themselves. So, yes, we gave chase, but it was with Mila's wellbeing in mind that we set off after her."

Her rage levels rising, Mila wasn't sure how many more of Thomas' lies she could listen to. No matter what she threw at him, he batted it away with ease, always making himself and Unlimited Horizons sound like they were angels taking care of humanity's downtrodden.

"I want to see my sister," she growled.

"Yes," Thomas nodded, his voice filled with sadness. "I know you do, and you know why we have kept you at arm's length. Talia came here to escape the life that led her to drink and drugs. You were part of that life, Mila."

"Why you …" Mila surged forward, looking like she might gouge out Thomas' eyes if she could get close enough.

Albert's tight grip on her shoulder held her in place.

"However, since you have all these reporters and cameras with you, I think the only sensible course of action is to accept defeat and hope you don't damage her progress too badly."

Chapter 24

They were led to the main administrative building, where a nervous-looking middle-aged man in a linen shirt was waiting at the entrance. He had the harried appearance of someone who had been suddenly thrust into a situation he was woefully unprepared for, like a vegetarian accidentally wandering into a butchers' convention.

"I am Stefan," he announced, his German accent thick enough to spread on toast. "I am the spiritual guidance counsellor here. You wish to see Talia Petrov, yes?"

"Yes," Mila said, her lips tight. She refused to add a 'please' to the end of her reply. After so much time in the camp trying to achieve this one single task it made her angry that they would give in so easily now. It made it seem as though all her claims were exaggerated.

"She is in afternoon meditation now. We have sent someone to fetch her," Stefan explained, gesturing for them to follow him. "Please, this way."

Stefan led them through the building, turning right as they entered the foyer to use a corridor Albert failed to venture down in either of his previous visits. It led to a door at the very end and passing through it they accessed a part of the camp they hadn't seen the previous night.

It was shielded from view by fences and buildings, but there was no doubt in Albert's mind that he'd now entered the inner sanctum of the community. The area outside with the accommodation and people was just the arrivals lounge. It was tidy and pleasantly landscaped, but this was the part of the camp Mila had been unable to reach.

Walking backwards with Bruno and Thomas either side of him, Stefan held out his arms to stop the advancing squad of reporters and cameras.

"To protect the privacy and anonymity of our residents, I feel I must remind you that they all came here to escape the pressures of the outside world and the constant, unavoidable media. I must ask that you go no further. You can see all that there is to see from here."

Whispering so Albert would hear, Roy said, "But what can't we see?"

There were restricted areas they would dearly love to access, but there was no hope of sneaking off to explore. Albert could see the digital security badge on Bruno's jacket. Thomas had one too, but Stefan did not.

Speaking to Mila, Stefan said, "Talia is being prepared and will be out soon." Addressing the journalists, he added, "Please feel free to film, but I must insist that you do not bombard Talia Petrov with questions. She has made great progress here and I will not expose her to unnecessary outside influences." He ran out of things to say, but continued to watch the visitors, his eyes stopping when they met Albert's.

It lasted for only a moment, but the distrust Stefan felt was projected and it made Albert think he truly believed in what he was doing. The claims he made weren't just words to the spiritual guidance counsellor and, if it was true, the people at Unlimited Horizons had helped Talia break free from her addictions. That was to be commended, even if it was part of something criminal.

Forced to wait, the journalists directed their cameras at the grounds and the people working it. Trim lawns, raised beds in which winter vegetables grew, and neat paths crisscrossed an area that stretched into the distance. The disused airfield lay beyond, and a thick forest sprouted beyond that. The old RAF camp had to cover hundreds of acres.

Albert could have asked Roy how big it was, how many miles of fence went around it, but the answers were insignificant.

Rex sat next to his human and sniffed the air. Only the vaguest notion of the panther's musky scent carried on the light breeze. It was here, it might even be watching, but Rex couldn't see it or pinpoint its location. The same could be said for Cerberus and Hades, the Doberman guard dogs. They were also being kept out of sight.

The camp smelled of freshly turned soil and grass clippings. Rex could smell rabbits nearby, but they were in their burrows now, the odour reaching his nose left by their recent nocturnal activities.

Residents moved around, but all in the distance as if cleared away so the journalists couldn't get to them. Albert could see some gardening, their manual tools moving slowly with the unhurried pace of the truly relaxed. Others sat on benches or chairs, either in groups or by themselves. Some appeared to be reading.

Ten minutes ticked by but just when Mila was about to protest, a figure she recognised appeared from a building to their left.

"Talia!" she gasped, detaching herself from the pack of reporters, and from Albert's side to rush forward.

Stefan moved to stop her, only to find Bruno barring his path. Albert watched the bigger man slowly shake his head and whisper something that made Stefan relax.

Mila ran, relief powering her body as she raced to reach her sister. Talia was among a group of other, similarly dressed residents being led by a woman in a cheap suit. They were chatting among themselves for the most part, but were clearly primed to see the cameras and reporters aimed their way.

Talia detached herself from the group, standing alone and operating independently. The optics were perfect, Albert acknowledged. Having accused Unlimited Horizons of holding her captive and keeping the sisters separate, they were showing them that nothing could be further from the truth.

In full view of his assembled press, Talia Petrov walked freely, a sort of sad smile on her face when she saw Mila. Where Mila looked dishevelled and desperate, Talia was the picture of serenity. Her hair was neatly braided, her simple linen clothing clean and pressed. She moved with the careful deliberation of someone who has learned to be mindful of every step.

She opened her arms, letting the younger sister come to her.

Mila wrapped her into a tight hug, holding on as though she worried Talia might evaporate or float away if she let her go.

"We need to hear what they are saying," Dieter insisted.

Thomas acknowledged his words with a nod. "Let's get closer, but please respect their privacy."

Albert smirked. The press were not known for doing any such thing, but they walked rather than ran to get closer to the sisters and they kept quiet so their words might be heard.

Not that the sisters were saying anything yet.

"Talia," Mila finally whispered, her voice breaking. She released her sister from the tight embrace and stepped back a pace.

"Mila?" Talia replied, her composed façade cracking slightly. "What are you doing here?"

"I followed you."

"Followed me?"

"Yes, Talia. You left me a note and disappeared," Mila sobbed. "I was so worried. Why didn't you answer my calls? My messages?"

"I needed to disconnect," Talia said, her voice soft but firm. "The digital world was poisoning me, Mila. You know how bad things were for me. Here, I've found peace. I'm clean for the first time in years."

Albert watched the interaction carefully. There was genuine affection between the sisters. Dieter and the other journalists observed silently, taking notes. Stefan hovered, visibly uncomfortable with the emotional scene.

"Talia, I don't think this place is what you believe it is."

A light frown creased Talia's forehead. "What do you mean?"

"I was here for eight weeks, Tal. Did they even tell you?"

Talia's frown deepened. "You were here? In the camp?"

Stefan chose to interject. "You were recovering from alcohol and drug addiction, Talia. We would have reunited you when the time was right, but we agreed the best thing for you was to ensure your recovery continued."

"I didn't agree to that," snapped Mila.

Thomas dipped his head to accept what she said, but countered with, "But your concerns were entirely secondary to your sister's needs. Had we told Talia you were here, she would have wanted to see you. We could not risk the potential impact an influence from her old life might have had."

Turning away from him, Mila said, "They wouldn't let me see you. They put me in a cell when I tried to find you and they chased me with dogs and motorbikes when I tried to escape."

"I don't understand," Talia gripped her sister's hands. "Why would you try to escape? This place is everything to me. You should join me here. It is so peaceful."

Mila glanced at Albert. In the car before arriving, they discussed strategies. Mila wanted only for her sister to leave, but revealing all they suspected would tip their hand and warn Horst when they wanted him kept in the dark if possible. He was almost certainly running a criminal operation behind the scenes, but it wasn't down to them to prove it.

Albert's great concern was to what lengths Mila might go to convince her sister to leave. She could blurt everything in her desperation to make Talia see the truth, so when she glanced his way, he gave a small shake of his head: now was not the time.

Gripping her hand, Mila said, "Talia, I want you to listen to me. This place, this community is not what you think it is. The people who come here are having their identities stripped from them …"

"I know, Mila." Talia smiled at her younger sister. "It's okay. In fact, it's good. Stripping us back to our simplest form allows us to be reborn as better people. I have digitally ascended and I'm better for it. There is no pressure here."

"No," Mila begged, "You're not listening to me. This place is dangerous."

Talia frowned again, but this time with the look of an adult listening to a particularly ridiculous child. "Mila, this is the safest place I have ever been."

Dieter stepped forward, taking his cameraman with him. Stefan wanted to stop him and this time Bruno and Thomas did nothing to prevent the smaller man from getting in his way.

It made no difference though, Dieter had interviewed politicians, gangsters, and killers. He wasn't about to be deterred by a guidance counsellor.

"Talia," he called. "Talia Petrov, by now you will have seen the cameras. Your sister's search for you has become a human-interest story that others will want to hear about. Are you able to leave if you want to?"

Surprised by the question, Talia said, "Yes. I think we are all able to leave if we so choose, but why would any of us want to?"

"So there is nothing keeping you here?"

"No."

Dieter threw a look at Albert before firing his next question. Albert was expecting it. He'd oversold the story. How else was he to get the press to attend? They came hoping for a big scoop that would lead the headlines but were now finding there was nothing here to justify their effort.

Stefan waved his arms in front of the camera. "That's enough. I'm afraid I cannot allow this to continue. Talia is at a delicate stage of her recovery."

"It's okay, Stefan," said Talia, disarming his argument completely when she added, "I am strong enough to answer some questions."

Dieter pressed her to tell the cameras how long she had been at the camp, what her treatment involved, and how she felt now that she knew her sister had been trying to reach her for so long. Talia handled it all with dignity, never once suggesting anything wrong on the part of Unlimited Horizons. If anything, her endorsement was the best advertising the spiritual retreat could get.

Albert could see Bruno and Thomas smiling as they exchanged whispered comments.

All the while Mila held her sister's hand, unwilling to let it go until Dieter asked his last question.

"Talia, your sister came here to take you away, to take you home. Do you wish to leave with her?"

Talia looked at Mila with apology etched on her face. She shook her head and said, "No. I'm sorry, Mila, but I need to stay here."

A tear ran down Mila's right cheek. "Oh, Talia ..."

"I think you have heard all there is to hear," said a new voice. It was one Albert knew, and he turned to see Mayor Horst Schultz marching across the lawn with Sabrina Aldridge in his shadow.

Chapter 25

The cameras swung around, the reporters rushing to be first with their question.

Raising his hands to shoulder height and making shushing motions, Horst Schultz expertly managed their expectations. "Ladies and gentlemen, if you please." He waited for them to fall silent, obeying his wordless instruction. Only then did he lower his hands back to his sides. "Thank you," he said, roving his eyes along the line of microphones to meet as many eyes as possible.

Sabrina stepped in close behind his left shoulder, whispering something before stepping back again.

"I want to thank you all for coming," the mayor of Hoffenholen said, although Albert doubted it was even slightly true. "This unexpected visit comes at the hand of someone who has chosen to target our facility." He drew attention to Albert in the centre of the front line. "Mr Albert Smith, a renowned sleuth known best for bringing a troubled member of the British royal family to justice, was right to raise concern when he met Mila Petrov, but as I am sure you have all now seen, her sister, Talia, is not only alive and well, but thriving here in our care. Talia just expressed her desire to remain with us, and I believe that concludes your business here. This is a private facility and home to persons who seek sanctuary from the modern world. I have permitted this intrusion because it served a purpose and because I know better than most the tenacity of the press." He smiled broadly as though he'd made a joke they all ought to share. "Now, though, it is time for you to leave. Our residents deserve the peace we promised them and have worked hard to earn the right to be free of the pressures modern-day living with its constant connectivity presents." Speech over, Mayor Schultz, the facilitator of Unlimited Horizons, walked away.

Thomas and Bruno, with Stefan lurking behind them, indicated the direction the press should go.

For a moment, Albert thought they might argue, but there really was no story for them to tell. From their perspective, it was a bust and they would be returning to their editors and producers empty handed.

It was a bust for Albert too. He thought Talia would go with Mila. That would have been good enough for him. To investigate further would be to invite danger he didn't need. He wasn't trying to be a hero. Not really. There was a crime happening under his nose and he felt driven to stop those behind it, but for once he accepted that his son made a valid point about his age.

If he could dig up something else, he would pass it to Melanie and her boss, Superintendent Hope. Otherwise, even though Mila still didn't have her sister, it was probably time for him to move on.

Following the press as they packed their gear and trudged toward the camp's gates, he kept his thoughts to himself.

The local police were massed at the gates, five patrol cars parked on the grass on the opposite side of the road. There were officers at the gate, talking to the guards, and more along the road between the press vehicles. Chief Kramer was inside the camp, standing next to another patrol car with a driver behind the wheel. He eyed Albert with an unreadable expression.

There were residents visible on this side of the camp, the side Mila never managed to get beyond, and Albert thought perhaps he recognised a few of the faces from the briefing he crashed. These were the new arrivals, the ones whose names he found in the mayor's office. They were yet to digitally ascend but would transition through to the other part of the camp in time. Would they ever come out again? Were they being used as part of a scam? They watched from a distance but made no attempt to approach the circus traipsing toward the exit.

Eager to leave now they believed there was no story, the journalists were moving faster than Albert. Not that he dawdled, but there being no reason to hurry, he walked at a pace at which his sore body wouldn't protest.

Rex padded along at his side, his tail swishing left and right.

"Mr Smith."

Albert twitched at the sound of his name being called by the mayor.

"Might I have a word, Mr Smith?"

Stopping where he was, Albert watched the press depart the camp through the open gate. They were done and would soon be on their way. They had served their purpose, even if the outcome was not the one he hoped for or expected.

"Mr Smith," Horst called again. He was behind Albert and waiting for the older man to face him.

When Albert shuffled his feet around to meet the politician's eyes, he found him much closer than he'd thought. The Unlimited Horizons' facilitator was practically standing on Albert's toes. Very much inside Albert's personal space, he still sported his election-winning smile, but it didn't reach his eyes.

When Albert refused to take a step back, Horst did, his eyes dropping to take in Albert's dog.

"He appears to have a slight limp, Mr Smith. Could it be that he has suffered an injury?"

Albert narrowed his eyes. "Such is life. Rex is an adventurous sort. He gets into all sorts of scrapes."

Horst nodded, his eyes never leaving Rex. "Indeed. My own pet suffered an injury last night. There were intruders in the camp and one of them delivered a wound using a sharp weapon. A blade of some kind. Like a sword, in fact."

Albert said nothing.

Lifting his eyes, the mayor looked at Roy and Beverly. They had stopped at the same time as Albert and were standing just a couple of yards away. Mila was with them, but she had tears slowly running down her face and seemed oblivious to everything happening around her.

"That cane conceals a sword, does it not?" Horst asked, though it wasn't so much a question as an accusation. "I have seen similar in my travels. It seems like such a coincidence, wouldn't you say, Mr Smith?"

Albert didn't like lying; it didn't suit him, and he'd never been very good at it. Keeping with a policy of sticking to the truth, he said, "I can assure you that whatever injury your pet sustained, it did not come at the hand of Roy Hope."

The mayor considered Albert with curiosity, taking a moment to consider his words before saying something Albert wasn't expecting.

"How much do you know, Mr Smith?"

A chill crept up Albert's spine. It was an admission of sorts, but not one he could use. More than anything, it was a threat. Horst believed Albert was on to him and now considered him to be a problem worthy of attention.

How was he supposed to answer? Caught off guard once again, Albert could only hold the mayor's gaze while he formulated a response. If he said the wrong thing, he would tip him off and the last thing he wanted was for Horst Schultz to vanish with his ill-gotten gains before the authorities could build a case and snatch him.

Choosing his words carefully, Albert said, "I know I saw a desperate woman being chased through the woods by dogs and men on motorcycles. I know her fate would have been very different had she been caught. I know she is right to be concerned about her sister, and I know stripping people of their identities is for your purposes and not theirs. I don't know what you are up to here, Mayor Schultz, and I have no desire to find out. I'm just a man touring Europe with some old friends and I bid you good day."

Leaving the mayor where he was, Albert clicked his tongue to get Rex moving and strode purposefully toward the gate with Roy, Beverly, and Mila at his side.

It was time to leave.

Chapter 26

In the car, Rex leaned into his human. The old man was distracted, his thoughts elsewhere, but he had an arm around Rex's shoulders and the two of them were always content to just share the other's company.

He looked out of the window, watching the trees go by. They passed a field of cows, all of whom were lying down in anticipation of the storm's arrival. Rex could smell the rain. It was miles away still, the clouds massing to the east were taking their time, but it was coming and would bring with it the kind of rain that would clear the gutters and wash the streets clean.

To Albert's right, Mila dabbed at her eyes with a tissue. Albert's plan to storm the camp using journalists as a spearhead was genius. It should have worked. It did work, but not for Mila. Talia was supposed to leave with her, that was the point, but she refused to listen and insisted that she needed to stay.

Mila knew she would change her mind if she knew the truth and that was why she slipped the prepared note into her pocket when they were hugging. Talia would find it and when she learned what was really going on, the situation would change.

In the front of the car, Roy and Beverly kept their thoughts to themselves. Beverly believed it was time to call it quits. Their return to Hoffenholen had been anything but the trip down memory lane she expected. Stress interrupted her sleep, and their meals, which should have been a joy, had been hurried and easily forgotten in the blur of Albert's latest investigation.

She loved her neighbour, but it was his late wife who she befriended and without her to keep Albert in check, he was cavalier with his safety. The knock-on effect that generated was her husband being cavalier with his. Last night proved to be a prime example. They could both have been hurt. They went up against a panther for goodness sake.

Once they returned to the hotel, she was going to take Roy to the bar where she would express in very certain terms that they were leaving. Together they would approach Albert, and she hoped he would see sense and leave with them. That had been the original plan – they were going to travel around for a few weeks and Albert was to join them for some of it.

Mila was the challenge, so far as Beverly could see. The poor girl was all alone and wouldn't want to abandon her plan to get her sister back. But what else could she do? They forced the hands of the people looking after her, but Talia chose to stay. Surely that was the end of it.

In the passenger seat, Roy didn't know what to think. He didn't need to hear his wife say it to know she wanted to move on. His thirst for adventure had never sat well with her and her tolerance for his 'silliness' as she would often call it in private, had diminished over the years. He couldn't say that he blamed her.

The previous night's race through the woods had left him feeling older today than he had in years. He was keeping quiet about it, but his lower back, his knees, his ankles … most of his body ached from the extreme exertion and he cursed getting old. He didn't like it, but Roy recognised they were out of their depth. He wanted to support Albert, goodness knows the man didn't get any from anyone else, but was it right to continue helping when it might be better all round for them to perform a tactical withdrawal?

Had Albert known what anyone else was thinking, he probably would have voiced his own thoughts aloud. Mila wasn't going to like it, but it was time to walk away. She couldn't help her sister, not if she didn't want to be helped, but what concerned him more was the mayor's decision to speak with him just as they were leaving. He could have let them go, but he didn't. Instead, he reinforced what Chief Kramer suggested; that they knew full well he was the intruder who broke into the camp. He saw Roy's cane with its concealed sword and clearly believed he was behind the panther's injury.

What was he going to do about that?

Ultimately, he needed to accept defeat. Any other course of action would place his friends, Mila, and Rex in jeopardy. If anything happened to any of them, he wouldn't be able to live with himself.

No one spoke a single word on the ride back to their hotel, Beverly taking them there without considering an alternate destination. It was midafternoon and the sun was already setting. One might consider that it was too late in the day to set off for pastures new, but that was precisely what Beverly wanted to do. All she had to do was pack and check out of their accommodation. They could be somewhere new in time to eat dinner. The sooner she left Hoffenholen behind the better.

Only when she applied the handbrake did Mila break the silence.

"What do we do now?" she asked.

Prompted to speak when neither of the men opened their mouths, Beverly didn't hesitate to tell her what she thought their next step should be.

"But my sister is still in there," Mila replied, her voice miserable.

"Because she chose to stay," Beverly pointed out. "She's an adult, Mila. She has the right to make her own decisions, and I witnessed her do precisely that."

"But she's been brainwashed. You must know that!"

Beverly glared at her husband. She shouldn't be the only one speaking. "Come on, Roy. Are you going to back me up on this?"

"Well …"

Beverly swung her eyes to the back seat where she pinned Albert in place. "You must have an opinion, Albert."

Albert gripped the door handle, getting ready to open it. "I think it might be best if we conduct this discussion inside." He opened the door and swung his legs out.

"Well, you lot can go ahead. The fuel light just came on and I'm going to fill the tank. I've had my fill of Hoffenholen, so if you boys wish to continue playing this silly geriatric detective game, you can do it without me. When I get back, I'm driving to Krefeld. That's where I'm staying tonight."

"My love," Roy began.

"Don't you try to sweet talk me, Wing Commander Roy Hope. That silly nonsense got me pregnant two weeks before our wedding night. It's still a wonder my mother didn't question why the baby was so big when it came two weeks early." Softening slightly, she cupped his chin with her hand. "I'm scared, Roy, and I want to go somewhere I can feel safe."

How was he supposed to argue with that?

Albert encouraged Rex out of the car and walked a few feet away to wait for Roy. Mila got out from the other side of the car, standing up to look over the roof at Albert with imploring eyes.

They both shut the back doors, leaving Beverly to discuss the terms of Roy's surrender. The first spots of rain were beginning to fall.

Mila said, "Albert, I can't give up on her."

Albert expected as much. "I understand, but …"

"It's okay," Mila cut him off. "This was never your fight, and you have done more than anyone could have asked. I don't know what my next move should be, but I am ready to continue alone. Beverly is right; you should go to Krefeld. Or wherever you want. Maybe it isn't safe here."

Albert wasn't about to decide either way, even though he knew both Mila *and* Beverly were right. He skirted the back end of the car, keeping his eyes away from the front seats where the long-married couple were now arguing with some volume.

He would straighten things out when they calmed down, but whatever he decided, Albert thought it best his friends departed as soon as possible. Behind him, a car door closed with a little more force than was necessary and he twisted his head to see Roy coming his way. He hadn't slammed the door – Albert didn't think his friend would ever do that, but the conversation had not gone well, and he felt bad that his need to help a woman in distress had caused such grief.

Mila paused in the doorway, poised to ask a question when Albert's phone began to ring. Rummaging in his coat pocket, he located it.

It was Gary calling again.

Chapter 27

"It's Gary," he announced, accepting the call. "One moment, son. I'm in a public area. Give me a moment to get to my room."

Unclipped from his lead and sent ahead, Rex bounded up the stairs, waiting at the top with his tail wagging until the older humans caught up.

Once they were in his room and had the door shut, Albert tapped the icon for the speaker and set the phone on the desk.

"Hello, Gary. I'm here with Roy and Mila."

"Dad," Gary wasted no time getting to the meat of his message. "I've got something for you on Sabrina Aldridge."

Albert straightened. "Go on."

"Her real name is Ásta Jónsdóttir. She's Swedish, not German. She's got a rap sheet and has served time, though her last spell inside was more than six years ago. It's all confidence schemes and scams to make people part with their money. Her arrests were always in Scandinavia, and it's all been small stuff, nothing so complex as what we've been discussing."

"Still, she's a criminal at heart," Albert remarked.

"I knew it," Mila growled.

Albert hushed her with a finger to his lips. "What else, Gary?"

"Well, she's probably in Germany illegally. Since Sabrina Aldridge isn't her real identity, I guessed it was stolen and that proved to be the case. The real Sabrina Aldridge is a German national. She has no children, is divorced, and vanished a little more than five years ago. There're no financial records beyond that point, but no missing person file was ever recorded because there was no one to miss her."

"She's taken the identity of a woman who surrendered it at Unlimited Horizons," Mila jumped to a hasty conclusion.

"We don't know that," Albert pointed out. "But you could easily be right."

"Anyway," Gary continued, "there's no record of Ásta Jónsdóttir entering Germany at all. Her passport was last flagged five years ago when she arrived in Switzerland."

"That's right around when Unlimited Horizons came into being," said Roy.

Albert asked, "Any connection to our friend the mayor?"

"Nothing concrete yet, but we're digging. Now you're not going to like the next bit."

Albert tensed, but said, "Go on."

"Her cell mate when she last went inside was the sister of the boss of the Halvorsen Clan. That's Sweden's top crime family; in case you were wondering."

Albert closed his eyes and exhaled slowly.

"Her brother, Alexander Halvorsen, is known as Ulv, which means 'the wolf'. He's not someone you want to mess with. We have nothing to link what you are seeing to the Halvorsen Clan, but it appears that Sabrina finished her sentence, left Sweden to fly to Switzerland, and not very long after that set up shop where you are. She's gone from petty crime to something far more sophisticated."

"So it's not a big leap to assume her cellmate gave her a few contacts and a way to rise in the criminal underworld," Albert finished what Gary was saying.

Sounding unhappy about it, Gary said, "Yeah. That's about the size of it. I've shared what we have with Europol and they're taking it seriously. The Bitcoin angle especially has their financial crimes unit interested. If this is what we think it is, we could be looking at one of the largest cryptocurrency frauds in European history."

"But you don't have enough for an immediate intervention." Albert wanted to confirm what he believed.

Gary sighed, the sound distorted through the phone's speaker. "No. Suspicion isn't enough, especially with a foreign national on German soil. We need more—transaction records, communication between conspirators, proof of identity theft. Something solid."

"Well, before you warn me to stay well away, I'll save you the bother. We went to the camp today."

"Dad!" Gary's exasperation was palpable even through the phone. "This isn't some small-town hustler or a petty thief. You've done your bit. Now let the professionals handle it."

"I hear you, son. That's what I'm trying to tell you. We went to the camp today with a busload of reporters. Mila is trying to get her sister back, and I saw a way to force them to let us speak with her. It worked, but her sister didn't want to leave."

Jumping on the point, Gary said, "It sounds like you've done all you can hope to do."

Mila looked sad but didn't argue.

"That's right, son." Albert felt bad too. "We're going to pack up and leave soon." Looking at Mila, he asked, "Just for my own sanity, and because by the time Europol cuts through the red tape, our friends at Unlimited Horizons might be long gone with their ill-gotten millions. How long do you need?"

A pause. "Three days, minimum. Probably more like a week."

"A week?" Mila protested, unable to keep quiet any longer. "If they get wind that anyone is on to them, they could be gone in hours. The note we found told us they have been transferring money out. They could have millions hidden away. Certainly, they have enough to live off for the rest of their lives."

"No, they don't," Albert argued. "There's no such thing for the greedy. Horst Schultz will wring every last penny out of this scam before he calls it a day. That's the one thing going in our favour. Also, if there is a mob connection to this Halvorsen Syndicate in Sweden, they will be the ones pulling the strings. Horst might be making a fat percentage off the top and laundering his residents' identities, but the involvement of a crime family likely means this is a money laundering scheme. They will be channelling multiple millions through their Bitcoin enterprise. The money isn't Horst's."

Hearing his dad's cogs turning, Gary snapped, "Dad, this is being handled! You need to back away."

"I already said I would, didn't I? Now that you have a known criminal in the midst of the camp, Europol should be able to act."

"But they won't. Not until they are sure they know what they are walking into."

Mila could scarcely believe what she was hearing. "What? We are talking about millions of Euros. We are talking about people's lives."

"But actually, we're not," Gary pointed out, matter-of-factly. "No one's life is at risk. Were that the case, things would move more smoothly, but according to my father, your sister, the very figure at the centre of your efforts, is choosing to stay of her own volition. There is no visible risk to life and no reason to believe the perpetrators are planning an imminent departure. From Europol's perspective, and this would be the same for any other agency examining the case, there is no desperate sense of urgency."

Albert placed a hand on Mila's shoulder and mouthed that his son was right. It wasn't what she wanted to hear but nothing was going to change any time soon.

"Well good luck with it, Gary. Let us know when something happens."

"So, you're leaving there tonight?"

"Tonight, or in the morning."

"Tonight, would be better, Dad."

Not willing to argue the point, Albert said, "Understood." They ended the call, and Albert slipped his phone away. He almost took it out again when he heard it ringing again almost immediately. He figured Gary had remembered something important, but it wasn't his phone ringing, it was Roy's.

Staring at it, Roy said, "Oh. I thought it was going to be Beverly. She hates filling the fuel tank and usually gets me to do it. It's some local number, though." He was about to stuff it back into his trouser pocket when Mila lunged for it.

"No! It's probably Talia!"

Chapter 28

Sensing how excited the humans were, Rex got to his feet and paced across the room to nudge his human's hand. Albert rewarded him with a few scratches behind his ears, but he didn't look down.

The call was cut off when Mila tried to grab it and accidentally hit the red button to reject it. Now she had both men staring at her. A rumble of thunder accentuated the tension everyone felt.

"What do you mean, 'It's probably, Talia'?" Albert asked. "How can she be calling? No one in the camp has a phone."

"I'm sorry," Mila blurted. "I didn't know what else to do. I was sure Talia would come with me, but just in case she didn't, I slipped a note inside her pocket."

"What did you tell her?" Albert demanded, though he suspected he already knew the answer.

Mila backed away a pace under his withering glare and when her calves hit the bed she stumbled backward onto it.

Outside, the storm built, flashes of lightning illuminating the curtains. Thunder boomed almost immediately afterward. The storm was right over them.

"I told her everything!" Mila wailed. "I had to! She needs to know who she is dealing with. It's all in the note. The identity theft, the involvement of the local police, the Bitcoin scam ... everything but the possible involvement of an organised crime family because I didn't know about it when I wrote the note. I told her to check for herself if she didn't believe me."

The phone rang again and this time they crowded around it. Mila pressed the answer button and said, "Hello?"

"Mila?" a frightened voice whispered. Even Roy and Albert recognised Talia's voice.

"Talia!" Mila squeaked. "Are you okay? You found my note?"

"How else would I know to call this number? Yes, I found the note. Listen, you were right. I'm underground and …"

"Wait," Albert cut in. "Do you mean in the bunkers beneath the base? You need to get out of there."

"Tell me about it. I found a terminal and it's so much worse than Mila wrote in her note."

Albert wanted Talia to head back to her room, wherever that was, and sit tight until the morning. They could figure out how to get her out of the camp then. Every minute she spent in the restricted area the more she was at risk of being discovered. Despite that, he couldn't fight his desire to hear what she had to say.

Her voice little more than a hint of noise as she exhaled, Mila said, "Go on."

Still whispering, Talia said, "I found a server room."

"It must be the same one I saw," Mila hissed.

"And there's a computer terminal at the back. It wasn't password protected, I guess they don't expect anyone to get down here, but I found a file on it called ID Sales and it lists all the people who have come to the camp. I know most of them and it looks like their identifications are being cloned and sold. Mine is on here, but it doesn't look like anyone had bought it yet. Yours is here too, Mila and it has been sold."

"What!"

"Shhh!" Talia urged. "There are people outside. I would have escaped already but I can hear them walking about. Your ID has been sold. That's if I'm reading this correctly. I don't know how this works, but that's what it looks like."

"Is there anything else?" Albert asked. "Any reference to money? Big numbers especially."

"Not that I have seen so far. Oh, wait. There're hundreds of files here. I'm working my way through them, but this one looks good. I ..."

A burst of loud voices filled the air, men shouting.

Mila shouted, "Talia!"

In the quiet of the hotel room, they heard Talia's panicked protests, a scream of fear, and the line going dead.

Her breath coming in stunned gulps, Mila ran to the bathroom to be sick.

Roy picked up his phone. "This changes things."

Albert said nothing. Things had changed. But what were they supposed to do about it? Talia was in trouble, and they could relay that to Gary. If he could then convince Europol or someone that she was in serious peril, maybe the timeline to intervention would shorten, but would anyone arrive in time to help Mila's sister?

Albert doubted it, but faced with the conundrum, the question remained the same: what could they do? Two old men, a dog with an injured backside, and a frightened young woman.

Mumbling, his hands not quite as steady as they had been, Roy said, "I need to call, Beverly."

While his friend did that, Albert checked on Mila. She hadn't eaten since lunch and had been so nervous about their imminent trip to the camp she only picked at food then. Her stomach now empty either way, she was swilling water around her mouth when Albert stuck his head around the doorframe.

"They're going to kill her, Albert."

"We don't know that."

"They're going to kill her and it's all my fault. I gave her the note. I told her she needed to check for herself. She got a security badge from someone and snuck into the bunkers just like I did. They caught her and it's my fault and they can't afford to let her leave!" Mila's voice reached a crescendo and ended with a desperate sob.

Albert grabbed her arms before she could collapse into a heap on the floor. She fell into him, allowing Albert to wrap his arms around her.

Rex followed them into the bathroom, giving comfort just by being there.

They were still there, Mila sobbing gently against Albert's chest when Roy came to the doorway a minute later. There was no trace of colour in his face.

"It's Beverly," he managed to stutter. "They've got her."

Chapter 29

Despite the noise of the storm, Albert had been able to hear Roy talking and assumed he was on the phone to his wife. That wasn't the case at all.

"Can you hear me, Mr Smith?" Horst's smooth tones filled the air. It was coming from Roy's phone and the name displayed on the screen was 'Beverly'.

His heart hammered in his chest, and he let Mila go without a thought to whether her legs would support her.

"I'm here," Albert said. "Am I to assume you have dropped the pretence?" Albert took out his phone and kept it in his hand, thankful no one at the other end could see what he was doing.

Sounding amused, the mayor said, "You can assume I am wise enough to keep my business private and that includes this phone call. You have caused me more bother than I could have anticipated, Mr Smith. Perhaps it is time that I addressed you less formerly. Would that be okay with you, Albert?"

"Oh, of course, Horst. Why, we're practically roomies now." Dropping the sarcastic tone, Albert let his anger take over. "You have something I want. Two things, actually. Give them to me and I will walk away. If I knew enough to act, I would have done so already. You probably think the authorities are closing in and they are, but you still have time to take the money and leave."

Horst Schultz laughed with genuine humour. "Leave, Albert? Why would I do that? I have nothing to fear from an investigation. You will come to me. You and that poisonous wildcat, Mila. And Mr Hope. I wish to speak with him about the injury my pet sustained."

"I already told you he had nothing to do with it."

"And by that I believe you mean that you are the guilty party. Either way, a car is about to arrive at your location. It will bring you to me and we will settle this matter. If you alert the police ... well, let's just say that wouldn't end well for two of my guests."

Albert wanted to argue. He wanted to threaten, but the mayor held all the cards. He could run, taking Roy and Mila with him, but he knew without asking that neither would go. A younger Albert might attempt to overpower the driver and use the car as a weapon to batter his way onto the base, but what then? It was a huge camp with many buildings and an underground bunker complex he couldn't hope to navigate.

If they wanted to see Beverly and Talia again, they were going to have to walk into Horst's trap.

A determined knock at the door preceded a boot kicking it open. Thomas and Bruno came through the door with guns in their hands. Rainwater dripped from their clothes.

"Ah, I believe I can hear your escorts arriving," chuckled the mayor.

Filled with rage, anxiety, and despair, Roy whipped the sword from his cane, sweeping it high in an arc above his head.

Bruno's silenced handgun coughed, the sound still loud in the confined space.

Crying out in pain, Roy fell backward, dropping both sword and the cane sheath it lived in.

Albert took a single pace toward his friend before realising his error.

Confused about what was happening, but aware the humans were displaying an unusual amount of negative emotions, Rex was fussing Mila when the door burst open. Two seconds later, Roy had been shot, and the dog was launching himself at the intruders. He could see their guns and knew the danger they represented.

Albert shouted, "Nooooo!" and threw himself into Rex's path.

Unable to change his trajectory, Rex slammed into his human, the pair colliding in mid-air.

An "Ooof," of air exploded from Albert's lungs, but he clung tight to his dog, threading his hand through Rex's collar to stop him from attacking the armed men.

Struggling against the pain, both from being winded by his dog and from slamming into the floor, Albert looked up at Bruno and Thomas while he hushed Rex and begged him to stop barking.

"It will be all right, boy," he cooed into Rex's ear. "This is not the right time."

Roy groaned.

"Roy?" Albert tried to sit up, taking three attempts to do so while keeping a tight grip on Rex.

Mila had crawled her way across the carpet to check on him.

"He's okay," she reported. "It's not that bad."

With Mila helping, Roy levered himself into a sitting position. "That cad shot me in my right shoulder. I'll have a matching set of scars."

Albert remembered only too well the last time Roy got shot. He was with him then too. It brought the faces of Tanya and Baldwin to mind. He'd never seen Baldwin again after that night, but Tanya was still out there somewhere, evading justice and probably working for a new boss.

"On your feet, all of you," snarled Thomas, picking up Roy's sword. Without taking his eyes off the targets, he managed to slide it back into its sheath and tuck it into his belt.

"It's time to go," added Bruno.

Albert tried to grab his phone, but Thomas saw where his hand was heading and got there first. Using the heel of his boot, he crushed the device into the carpet, grinding it with a few twists that ensured it would never work again.

"And yours," Thomas aimed his gun at Roy.

Struggling to move - his left arm was clamped over the wound to his right shoulder - Roy gritted his teeth and surrendered his phone without comment. It wasn't as if they had a choice.

Yanking the silk pocket square from his jacket with bloody fingers, Roy passed it to Mila who tied it crudely around the wound. It wasn't going to do much, but it was enough to stem the bleeding for now.

They left the hotel via an emergency exit door at the end of the corridor, thus avoiding the front of the hotel where they would have to pass a member of staff and any guests who happened to be coming or going. They could yell and make noise to attract attention but that would just put other people in danger.

Rain lashed at them the moment they stepped outside, but the black Mercedes G-Wagon was parked less then ten yards away. Ordered to run, they hustled to the car and were bundled inside at gunpoint.

Rex twisted his head to check the two gunmen. He knew their scents from the very first encounter in the woods. When they rescued Mila, the men were on motorbikes and impossible to catch. That was no longer the case, and he could disarm one with a snap of his teeth. The second one, though … Bruno and Thomas were far enough apart that he couldn't get from one to the other swiftly enough to be sure he wouldn't get killed in the process.

Aware enough to know they were all being taken back to the camp where he would face the additional challenge of the Dobermans and, worryingly, the panther, Rex found his heart beating harder than he was used to. He was afraid. The unexpected and unwelcome emotion clawed at his confidence.

Ushered into the back of a large, black car by his human, Rex squeezed into one corner, trapped between the door and the old man's legs. Mila went in the middle and Roy settled uncomfortably on the far side of the back seat.

Thomas took the wheel with Bruno in the front passenger seat. He didn't bother with his seatbelt, leaving himself free to twist in his seat to better hold his gun on the trio in the back.

The gunmen were close enough now that Rex believed he could get them both. Especially since Thomas had tucked his gun away to take the steering wheel, but he no longer had the space, nor the freedom of movement to launch himself at them.

In the darkness, no one they passed gave the car a second glance. Thomas drove sedately, keeping to the speed limit and obeying the signs and signals until they were out of town and beyond the areas lit by overhead lights. Only then did he pick up the pace, though the rain demanded he keep his speed below fifty. Above that the windscreen wipers simply couldn't keep up.

Albert noted his reluctance to attract attention with interest. It conflicted with a theory he'd formed that morning when he met Chief Kramer but supported a new one he'd developed just a short while ago when talking to the mayor. Whether he was right or not, and what good that would do them came down to whether the phone call he surreptitiously made went through.

He'd felt for sure that Thomas or Bruno would notice his screen, but neither had. Not even when Thomas ground it to death with his boot.

Turning off the road and pulling up to the front gate of the old RAF base, Albert knew it was the longest of long shots, but at that moment, it was all he had.

The barrier swung open, and the car passed under it, taking Roy, Albert, Rex, and Mila into the lion's den for the second time that day.

His voice quiet, and intended only for his own ears, Roy said, "I'm coming, my love. I'm coming."

The emotion captured in his words tore through Albert's heart. He'd led them all to this end. The need to correct injustice wherever he found it. The desire to test his detective skills … Hubris. Hubris led him to believe he could take on a man who held all the cards. Sure, he'd chosen to walk away, but too late for it to do them any good.

The car didn't stop at the headquarters building as Albert thought it might. Thomas kept going, driving around the accommodation buildings to a point beyond where he pulled up close to a wide, imposing door. It was made from thick steel and probably built to withstand a nuclear blast. Albert held no doubt it would lead down into the warren of underground rooms beneath the camp.

Mila confirmed it. "This is where I got in," she said.

A pinprick of green light shone from a small panel to the right of the door. The security panel.

Bruno waited for Thomas to exit the car and retrieve his gun before sliding backward off his seat, the barrel of his handgun never leaving the backseat.

"End of the line," Bruno said.

"Figuratively and literally," added Thomas with a light snort of amusement.

Bruno motioned with his gun. "Get out."

Chapter 30

They complied, Mila helping Roy. His face was pale, the combination of pain and shock taking him to the edge of unconsciousness. His feet dragged a little, and his head lolled, but there was no point asking if they could take a break or let him recover. Albert worried they were as likely to shoot him and finish the job as they were to help.

The rain fell in sheets, soaking through their clothes in the few seconds they were outside.

Thomas held his security badge against the lock and the door slid slowly open with a soft beep. They were all glad to get out of the storm.

Inside, the corridor was bare concrete but polished to a smooth finish. It was seven feet high and maybe six feet across; wide enough to carry equipment inside and down to whatever the original designers built it for. Overhead fluorescent lamps, the six-foot tube type from a time when the camp was built, filled the space with light. To the right as they entered were old warning signs advising those entering of the precautions they should take. At another time, Albert might have found them interesting to read.

Thomas led the way with Bruno bringing up the rear. Both had their weapons drawn and held ready should their prisoners choose to do something foolish.

Thirty yards in they turned right at the end of the concrete tunnel to find a set of steps leading down.

Leaning in, Mila whispered, "Down there is where I found the server room. That must be where they caught Talia."

"No talking," snarled Bruno, halting Albert's response before it could form.

They descended the stairs, Roy gasping and panting as he fought waves of nausea and fainting spells. Albert trusted Mila to keep him upright. He could see Rex watching Bruno and Thomas and couldn't risk lending a hand to look after Roy. If Rex tried, he would get one of their guards, but someone would get shot in the mayhem that followed.

Their situation looked dire, but until Albert knew for certain they were doomed, he couldn't risk a strategy that might get someone killed.

Along another wide corridor and around a corner, they began to hear voices.

Drawing nearer, they became more distinct, and Roy mumbled, "That's Beverly."

Albert twisted his torso, looking back at his friend. Roy's face had more colour than when he last looked and he appeared to be leaning less heavily on Mila to keep him upright. What Albert could not tell was whether the old RAF pilot had been faking it to make himself look defenceless while looking for an opportunity to turn the tables.

He hoped not. For all their courage, they were old men. They might once have been fast and strong but compared to the young men holding guns on them, they might as well have been frail enough to need wheelchairs. It was a sad but unavoidable fact.

Turning yet another corner, Albert could see an open space where it ended. They were coming into a large room.

Rex had been able to smell the panther since they entered the underground bunker system. The Dobermans, too, and the scent grew stronger with each passing yard. His powerful nose also told him Beverly was ahead. So too Horst Schultz and the tall blonde woman they met yesterday when they first visited the camp. The scent of a third woman was one he'd only caught in passing. It belonged to the woman Mila exchanged hugs with a few hours ago when they came to the camp. Rex thought they were litter mates, though he couldn't be certain.

Reaching the end of the tunnel, they came into a room that was far bigger than Albert anticipated.

"This was the original war room," Roy murmured loud enough for Mila and Albert to hear. "I was only in here a couple of times. For war exercises, I guess you would call them. We would plot out possible attacks the Russians might employ, and role play how we would defend against them. It was pointless, really," he added. "We would have all been wiped out in a matter of minutes."

Thankful the Cold War never amounted to an actual conflict, Albert took in the scene stretching out before them. The large room was forty feet in either direction and at least fifteen feet high. It was all concrete with fat silver ducting running across the ceiling. Bare cables ran down the walls to switches that controlled the lights or heat or air conditioning, and there were shadows on the aluminium checker plate floor to show where machinery or computers – the old ones that were the size of a car – had once sat. It was all gone now, most likely cleared out to protect secrets when the base was emptied and sold.

In its place, in the centre of the floor was what looked like a boxing ring but without the ropes around the edges or the corner posts to which they would connect.

On the far side was a raised platform that looked to be part of the original installation. There, Mayor Horst Schultz sat on what Albert's brain instantly labelled as a throne. The wide wooden chair had a high back extending a foot above the mayor's head. Its dimensions dwarfed the man sitting in it, making him look small. Albert guessed that wasn't the effect he was going for.

On another day in a different situation, Albert would have poked fun, but the sense of dread in his gut stole his sense of humour. Sabrina Aldridge, or rather, Ásta Jónsdóttir, stood to the side of the throne. Her blonde hair and perfect features were once again marred by the unpleasant grimace on her face.

On two sides, a hand and knee rail protected a drop where the floor ended a yard or more from the wall. Albert couldn't see how far down it went, but took in everything as he tried to formulate some way in which they might escape. It looked hopeless, but he refused to think like that.

"Keep walking." Thomas jabbed him in the back with the muzzle of his gun, drawing a grunt of pain from Albert that made Rex growl.

Rex was on edge. The Dobermans, sitting to the right hand side of the mayor, looked down at him, their eyes boring into his. The panther was on the mayor's left, lying on a raised plinth, its long black tail twitching idly back and forth while it examined Rex with eyes that spoke of cruelty to come.

Three yards to the right, Beverly and Talia peered down between the bars of a large cage. A fat padlock held a small square door shut. The cage wasn't designed to house a human. With only four feet of head space, the women were both on their knees.

Seeing her husband, Beverly gasped, "Roy! Roy, darling. Are you okay?"

Roy offered her a tight smile. "It's just a scratch, my love."

Acting as though they hadn't spoken, the mayor rose to his feet, clapping his hands together gleefully as though being reunited with loved family members he hadn't seen for years.

"Wonderful. I'm so glad to have you all join me here."

A small snort left Albert's nose. They were taken from their hotel at gunpoint, yet the fool talked as if they were responding to an invitation.

When no one said anything, Horst stepped down from his raised platform, descending a short flight of stairs to reach the floor. For a moment he was lost from sight behind the canvas boxing ring. When he emerged, the politician's smile was back, and he advanced with his hand out as though Albert was going to shake it.

Rex was confused. He thought the man coming toward them was the bad guy. Beverly and Talia were locked in a cage – he could smell the fear coming from them – but he was acting friendly and talking to his human in a tone that suggested they were on good terms. Was he supposed to bite him or not?

Albert pulled Rex in tight by his side, and when the mayor's hand came close enough, he slapped it away.

"This is probably where I'm supposed to say something like 'You won't get away with it', but I don't think I'll bother. I mean, you won't get away with it, that should be obvious to anyone with half a brain, but it's clear you're not operating with a full deck."

Horst tipped back his head and laughed, the exaggerated reaction giving Albert the perfect opening. It had been a while since he'd punched someone, but he put his whole body into it and despite his advancing years, slowing reflexes, and reduced muscle mass, the uppercut to his exposed chin knocked Horst Schultz off his feet.

"Good one, Albert!" cheered Roy.

Bruno clubbed the back of Albert's neck with his gun, sending him to his knees.

Rex whipped around, snarling and lunging, his teeth coming within inches of Bruno's gun arm before he ran out of lead.

On his knees, Albert hung on for dear life. "No, Rex!"

Bruno's gun pointed right at Rex's skull. A twitch of the trigger and it would all be over.

Rex continued to bark and snarl. "*Let me go! He hurt you. Tell me to sic 'em!*"

Getting back to his feet, no trace of his smile remaining, the mayor snapped, "Get that dog under control, Mr Smith, or I will have him shot."

His head and neck a ball of pain, Albert looped an arm around Rex's shoulders and pulled him close.

"Not now, Rex," he whispered into the dog's ear. "Not now." He wanted to tell Rex to wait for the right moment, but he had no clue how they were going to get out of their current situation. They were in deep trouble, and no one was coming to save them.

With the old man's arms around him, Rex stopped struggling to get free and settled his backend onto the floor once more. He wanted to chase and bite but his human hadn't given him the command.

Horst was waiting for Albert when he got back to his feet.

"That was a good punch, Albert."

"Thank you. I have several more like it if you'd be so kind as to stand still while I hit you again."

Horst laughed mirthlessly. "I think not. Brawling is so ugly. To me it is the method of the uneducated, the unrefined. I am disappointed you would stoop so low."

"You're disappointed? Why should I care? You brought us here to kill us, didn't you? You're worried the Bitcoin scam you have running with Ásta Jónsdóttir over there …"

Sabrina flinched at the sound of her real name being used.

"Yes," said Albert, "I know who you are. So do Europol. They'll be here soon."

"But not soon enough," Horst replied, sounding confident. "And when they do arrive, they won't find anything that will incriminate me. The beauty of cryptocurrency is how easy it is to move. And to hide."

Still up on the raised platform by the throne, Sabrina asked, "How does he know my name, Horst? How can he possibly know my name?"

Albert sneered, "I'm a detective, you silly girl. Sabrina Aldridge is a stolen identity. You have these poor fools surrender all their cards and IDs when they enter your facility. Then you sell them, right? To criminals, I assume. Except not all of them. Some you use to underpin the Bitcoin operation. Their names are on it, right. Digital fingerprints, signatures, and even money in their bank accounts because you have control of those too. If the authorities were to launch an investigation, it would be some of the residents here they would arrest because you have made it look like they are behind the money laundering scheme." The how and the why had pieced itself together in the car. Talia's revelation was the final clue. The digital ascension thing had always smelled like utter nonsense, and it was. They wanted their identification so they could use it.

"Is it crime money, Horst?" Albert figured he might as well go for broke. If he was wrong about his part of it, it really wouldn't matter. "Did Sabrina come to you with a clever plan to launder millions of euros of organised crime money?"

Sabrina couldn't hide her horror. "How does he know that?" she screeched.

"You are most astute, Albert," said Horst, his tone suggesting he meant the compliment. "Truly you deserve the attention the press gives you. But you were wrong about one thing. I didn't bring you here to be killed."

Albert almost had to shake his head to clear it. Had he heard the man correctly?

"Were that the case Thomas and Bruno would have done the deed back at the hotel. No, Albert, as I said when we first met, I am a gentleman. You are here to settle a matter in a gentlemanly manner. Not with fists, Albert, but with something far more befitting of our status."

Sabrina, who had descended the platform to join Horst on the war room floor, tugged at his arm. "We don't have time for this. If he knows then the outside world also knows. I'm not going to jail again, Horst."

"You should probably stop breaking the law then," Albert suggested.

Sabrina shot Albert a hate-filled look and tugged at Horst's arm again. "We have to go."

Horst didn't even bother to look her way. "You go. I have business here. When it is concluded I will still be mayor. It is an election year, and I am going to win. I have brought prosperity to this small town, and they love me for it."

Sabrina stared at him for a moment, her mouth hanging open, but when he continued to ignore her, she walked away, her heels click, clicking on the concrete floor as she hurried from the chamber.

"Now then, Albert. I need to confirm one thing before we start."

"What's that?"

"Was it really you who injured Raven? Or was it Mr Hope?" He flicked his eyes to look at Roy.

"The panther?" Albert checked who they were talking about. "It was me. He was going to kill my dog." He could see no reason to lie about breaking in. Horst clearly wasn't buying it, anyway.

The mayor nodded. "Very well. That is better, I think. Had Mr Hope been the guilty party, you would have had to fight in his place. His injury would give me too much of an advantage."

Stepping forward, Roy spat, "I'll fight you, you cad."

"No. I shall fight Albert. But I will ask that he be permitted to wield your weapon. It is fitting, no?"

Thomas offered Horst the cane.

Drawing in a deep breath, Albert crouched to bring his face level with Rex's.

Rex looked at his human. "*What's happening?*"

"I have to go now, Rex. I want you to stay with Roy and Mila, okay?"

Rex knew something was wrong. Beyond the terrible situation they found themselves in, that is.

"*Where are you going? You make it sound like you are not coming back.*"

Albert put his arms around his dog and hugged him tightly. "Be a good dog now, okay? If you get the chance to help Roy and the others, make sure that you do so."

Looking over Albert's shoulder as he hugged him, Rex found that he was facing the Dobermans, the pair of them looking down at him from their lofty perch.

"*You see?*" he whined at them. "*This is what it is supposed to be like with humans.*"

Albert handed Rex off to Roy with a final scratch of the fur around his neck and turned to face the mayor again.

The mayor of Hoffenholen removed Roy's thin blade from the cane sheath. Examining it, he turned it over and held it aloft so the overhead lights caught the edge. He swished it experimentally through the air, testing its weight and balance.

"A fine piece of craftmanship," he remarked. "Where was it made?"

"I bought it in Singapore," Roy said.

"Very good." Horst slid the blade back into the sheath and handed it to Albert. "Please, Albert, join me. We will settle this as gentlemen." He hopped up onto the canvas platform, stripping off his shirt to reveal bare skin beneath. "As a little added incentive, if you win, you and your friends will go free."

Albert choked on a laugh that held no humour. "That's a stupid lie."

Horst collected a sword of his own from the far side of the canvass. It was similar in many ways to the one Albert held, but it was longer and heavier and, more importantly, was being held by someone who knew how to use it.

"It's not a lie at all, Albert. As I have said many times now, I am a gentleman. I find the modern era shameful. People have no respect for themselves or for each other. They lie, they cheat ..."

"You're laundering money for an organised crime family while making a fat percentage off the top no doubt," Albert pointed out, undoing his shirt.

Horst conceded the point. "Regardless, if you beat me, you and your friends will go free. You have my word."

It was a cruel thing to tempt him with. He was a good twenty years older and though taller and with a longer reach, he'd not held a sword since a few fencing classes when he was a teenager. The prize was there to make sure he gave his best before the mayor grew bored of toying with him and ended it.

"To the death?" Albert confirmed.

"Is there any other way to end this?"

Horst probably meant what he said about letting them go, but if Albert somehow emerged victorious and he was dead, did the mayor really think Thomas and Bruno would let them go?

"Enough talking," Horst brought his sword down so the point rested just an inch above the canvas. "You injured my pet, Albert, and I demand satisfaction."

Albert dropped his shirt onto the dusty concrete floor and climbed onto the raised canvas platform. It gave a little, the floor designed to absorb impact from feet and bodies, just like a boxing ring.

Horst whipped his sword up and around so it pointed straight up in line with his body and directly between his eyes. Albert mimicked the move, returning the salute.

And then it was time for a duel.

Chapter 31

Unable to believe it was happening, Albert brought Roy's sword up. He held it with one hand, balancing his body with the other and tried to keep his knees bent and his feet light. He could recall none of what his fencing instructor taught him sixty years ago. In fact, the only thing he could remember was that he joined the afterschool club because he fancied Jenny Paxton and she was a member. Foolishly, he'd thought the shared interest would increase his chances, but she mocked his lack of ability and terrible footwork. He lost interest in her and quit the club.

How he regretted that now.

He circled, allowing Horst to come to him. It brought him in line with Beverly and Talia in their cage. Albert tried not to look, he knew he couldn't afford to, but he caught the look of horror etched into Beverly's face. She knew he was about to die, but then so did everyone else in the room, including Albert.

Horst lunged, thrusting his blade through Albert's defence to score with his first attempt. The tip of the sword dug into the flesh covering his ribs, six inches below his left nipple. An explosion of pain ripped through him and he cried out, ducking back to get away.

Horst could have followed the first strike with a second, easily winning the fight and ending it in less than thirty seconds, but he didn't. Just as Albert predicted, he wanted to play with him, like a particularly evil cat toying with a helpless mouse.

Albert didn't dare look down at the wound. He could feel his blood, warm, wet, and sticky, leaking from it to coat his abdomen.

Raising his right arm, he was thankful to find moving the sword around didn't hurt too badly.

Horst came again, madness in his eyes when he swung his blade through the air.

Albert turned, parrying the drive with Roy's sword, but Horst was moving it to take a second swing almost before Albert could register that he'd managed to block the previous one. He was on the back foot continuously, always going in reverse as Horst pressed forward.

The mayor would swing, Albert would block, desperately trying to be ready for the next move. Their swords clashed, the metallic sound the only noise in the room save for the gasps from the onlookers and the occasional murmur from either Bruno or Thomas as they enjoyed the display.

That changed when Rex started barking. Albert couldn't risk a glance to see what was happening, but assumed his dog was going nuts watching him fight and bleed. He didn't see when the pair of Dobermans got to their feet and walked around to take up flanking positions either side of the German Shepherd. They were five yards out and ten yards apart, standing just to the left and right of Thomas and Bruno.

To Beverly, stuck in the animal cage with Mila's sister, it looked as though they were getting ready to deal with the survivors when Albert fell.

Albert parried another blow, but sensing a small opening, moved forward to see if changing direction might throw Horst off balance. It did, but the result was that when their blades met they found themselves locked in a battle of strength. Their swords together, each gripping the other's arm with their non-sword hand, they pushed and strained.

But not for long. Slowly, the mayor of Hoffenholen pushed Albert's sword down. Once he had enough leverage, Albert knew Horst would be able to yank his arm free and strike a blow at either his chest or neck. To prevent that he had to let go.

He did just that, but in so doing left his right side open and just wasn't fast enough to get out of the way when a scything swing carved through the air to catch his ribs again.

Gritting his teeth, Albert fell back, his cry of pain bringing a glint to the mayor's eyes. More blood flowed, smears of it coating the canvas where they moved through it.

"You should never have come here," said Horst, his breathing laboured and his skin beginning to shine with sweat. "And you should never have interfered with my business, Albert." He thrust again, this time tagging Albert's right bicep.

This time the wound did affect his ability to wield the sword. A natural righty, he could still hold the blade aloft, but doing so was agony.

He backed away, Horst pursuing him. Albert knew he was going to die. There wasn't a thing he could do to prevent it and the grin on Horst's face told him the mayor knew it too. But a strange thing happened when he accepted his end was mere moments away.

An almost serene peace settled over him. He switched the blade from his right hand to his left, and just about managed to deflect the next blow. He stepped back, getting some distance and watching for an opening. The one time he'd changed direction and closed with the mayor the strategy had worked. Sort of. Albert believed he could get in close enough to deliver a blow, but the strategy he attempted to employ the previous time was the wrong one.

Settling himself, for he knew this was very much do or die time, Albert waited.

"I want to thank you, Albert. Having you killed would have been easy, but this is so much more elegant. For a man such as yourself, a man who has done great things, what better way to go out than on your feet, fighting for what you believe in? So much better than wasting away of some terrible illness a few years from now when your body simply isn't strong enough to fight any longer. We are gentlemen ..."

Horst swung his sword back, creating an opening, and Albert stepped into it. The sword came down, aimed at Albert's skull, but he blocked it with his own blade and kept moving forward. The last time he reversed direction he wanted to use his sword, but the fact was that he just didn't have the speed to beat the mayor.

What he did have, was dirty tactics.

The headbutt landed on the bridge of Horst's nose, splatting it with a satisfying crunch.

"You might be a gentleman," Albert yelled through his fear and pain, "but I was a police officer, and I learned to fight dirty a long time ago."

Horst stumbled backward, his non-sword hand to his face where blood flowed through his fingers. Wide eyes went even wider when Albert kicked him in the trousers.

Beverly cheered at the top of her lungs, a sound echoed by the rest of 'Team Albert'.

Stunned, Horst retreated with Albert stalking after him.

Albert swung, aiming to maim.

Horst stopped it. Even injured he was fast enough to parry Albert's blade.

Albert swung again, pursuing the mayor of Hoffenholen. He had an advantage, but it wouldn't last long.

However, Horst showed his true colours, panicking now that he was no longer in control.

"Kill them!" he screamed. "Kill them all."

Chapter 32

Bruno and Thomas raised their guns and the Dobermans leapt. Albert saw it all from the corner of his eye. He spun away from the mayor, exposing his back as he ran to get to Roy and Mila and Rex. He knew he couldn't get there in time, but he had to try.

Moving as fast as he could, his wounds screaming in protest, Albert leapt from the canvas, but hanging in mid-air, he watched the Dobermans defy his expectations. He thought they were going for Rex, so when instead they attacked Bruno and Thomas, he almost spat out his teeth.

When his human heard Rex barking, he didn't know it was a continuation of an argument his dog had been presenting since he first met the camp's guard dogs. Cerberus and Hades didn't know any different. Littermates since birth, they came to live at the compound as puppies more than two years ago. They weren't mistreated exactly, but there had never been any affection from the humans. They did as they were told and if they didn't do it quickly enough, Raven the panther punished them.

The sleek black cat was too powerful, too strong, and too dangerous for either dog to disobey, but Rex had shown them how different their lives could be. In him they saw all they were missing.

They had circled around behind the mayor's henchmen to look like they were waiting for the command to attack the prisoners. But when they saw Thomas and Bruno lift their guns, they went for their own handlers.

Raven lifted his head, momentarily confused by what he saw.

Both gunmen squealed in pain. Their guns went off, the sound like a shockwave it came so close to the Dobermans' faces, but they held on, pulling the men to the ground with their bodyweight.

Stunned by the turn of events, Roy and Mila saw the chance on offer and grabbed it with both hands. Bruno and Thomas still held their guns in their right hands. They were down on their knees, but still able to fight back. If they could swap their guns from one hand to the other …

Mila kicked Bruno in the ribs as hard as she could and went for his gun. Roy grabbed the cane sheath – Thomas dropped it when Hades bit his arm. A whack to Thomas' gun hand sent his weapon skittering across the floor, but the fight was far from over.

Rex found himself torn between running to help his human – the old man was covered in blood and breathing heavily – and getting into the fight to help Hades and Cerberus. His moment of indecision gave Raven all the time he needed.

The giant black cat leapt from the plinth next to Horst's throne, landed gracefully on the canvas, and bounded in one fluid movement to fly past Albert. Moving faster than anyone or anything else in the room, Raven looked like a shadow come to life. He landed on Hades' back, biting his head and gouging his fur with claws like a row of sickles.

The Doberman yelped, letting go of the arm he held to fend off an attack he never saw coming.

Raven clamped down harder on the dog's head. He needed to adjust his bite if he was to kill him right now, but all he really needed to do was injure him enough to take him out of the fight. Then it would be Cerberus' turn.

Rex slammed into Raven's ribs like a freight train.

Mila had Bruno's gun but couldn't get a clean shot at either man. Cerberus still held Bruno in his grip and thrashed his body from side to side, deepening the wound in the man's arm. Locked in the battle, he hadn't seen Raven attack his brother.

Knocked loose when the air rushed from his lungs, Raven rolled away. It took him to the edge of the railing. The drop the other side wasn't a long one – no more than a few feet, but when Rex hit him again before he could recover and regain his bearings, his back end slid out into free air.

Raven scrambled with his paws, but too much of his body was already hanging over the edge. Rex watched the panther fall, its rage-filled grimace aimed directly at him when it dropped out of sight.

Dismissing him, Rex looked for his human.

Albert wasn't anywhere in sight.

Roy wanted to get to his wife. The shock of his injury had faded, leaving him feeling weak, and in pain, but also angry and determined. One of the guard dogs was injured, the other had spat out Bruno's arm to go to his brother, but they appeared to somehow now be on their side and neither man looked inclined to get up and renew the fight. They were down and bleeding and Mila held a gun on them.

Shouting, the adrenalin fuelling his volume, Roy demanded, "Where are the keys?"

He took a step forward, angry enough to do violence if they didn't give him what he wanted, but a roar from the panther stopped him in his tracks.

Mila's eyes shifted away from Thomas and Bruno. She'd seen the panther fall, but the roar hadn't come from all that far away, so the giant cat was coming back and right now that made it the most dangerous thing in the room. She was the only one with a gun. Mila might not want to shoot an animal but doubted she would be given a choice.

Rex stiffened.

His nose had led him to find his human. Albert was lying on the canvas, the loss of blood, shock, and pain from his injuries just too much to fight. Rex couldn't tell how badly injured he was, or even if he was close to death. All he knew was that his favourite person needed help and he wasn't going to be able to give it.

The humans might not be able to tell what the panther said, but Rex knew and so did the Dobermans.

Rex twisted his head to see the cat's black head emerge above the edge of the floor and Hades barked, "*Run!*"

Raven leapt back onto the control room floor. The injury to his shoulder made his landing a little awkward – he favoured his right front leg where the sword wound undoubtedly hurt, but it wasn't about to slow him down.

Glaring at Rex, he said, "*And now I'm going to rip out your throat.*"

Rex needed no further encouragement. Twisting his body to face the other way, he pushed off with his back legs, put his head down, and ran.

It all happened in the blink of an eye, Mila loosing three shots at the panther when it streaked across the room in pursuit of Albert's dog. Each shot missed, gouging holes in the steel plate floor or concrete walls.

Seeing her distracted, Mila's aim no longer on him, Thomas launched himself off the floor. He slammed into her legs, knocking her backward so the fourth shot went wild and into the ceiling where it hit a light. Fragments of glass showered down as they struggled.

Bruno was half a second behind his partner, lunging to take out Roy before he could use his cane to stop Thomas.

Even injured the mayor's henchmen were going to be able to overpower Roy and Mila.

Roy fought Bruno for the cane, but the younger man had it clenched in the fist of his uninjured arm.

Cerberus, tending to his injured brother missed the struggle starting, but tearing himself away from Hades, discovered he was already too late to intervene.

Not too late for Roy and Mila to be saved. Just too late to be the one who saved them.

Chapter 33

Beverly had waited for the sword fight to start before trying to pick the padlock holding her and Talia inside the cage. Not that lockpicking was a skill she held within her arsenal. Yet once all eyes were focused on the cut and thrust of the two men on the canvas platform, what harm was there in trying?

Her handbag was still in the car, probably in the passenger footwell, she guessed, though it could still be on the passenger seat where she left it. Bruno and Thomas surprised her at the petrol station, grabbing her as she got back to her car.

The view from the small shop was obscured by their car, a high-sided Mercedes G-Wagon with blacked-out windows, so when Thomas came from behind her, the first time she sensed she was in trouble came when Bruno asked, "Does this smell like chloroform?"

A hand went over her mouth, the rag it held clamping over her nose and mouth. Sucking in a hard breath to fill her lungs so she could scream was the worst thing she could do. Of course, Beverly only realised that after the fact.

Waking up in the boot of her own car, she had kicked and screamed and banged on the boot lid to no avail. She believed there was a lever fitted somewhere that was specifically added to cars so people locked in the luggage compartment could escape. Was that real? Or just something she'd seen on TV? Either way, she couldn't find a lever, but as her fingers dug around, she did find a split pin. She even knew why it was in the boot.

Months ago, Roy had found a working model Spitfire plane for sale and insisted he had to have it. The model required some repair, but convinced he could fix it himself, they drove fifty miles to collect the infernal item. It was still sitting beneath an old blanket in their garage, where she imagined it would remain.

However, the box of bits it came with had spilled during the journey, and Roy clearly hadn't collected all the little parts when he said he had because she'd just found a split pin.

Easy to bend, it proved the perfect tool for opening the padlock. Talia expressed her shock when Beverly popped it open less than thirty seconds after manoeuvring her arms through the bars to fiddle with it.

No one noticed the women escaping their cage. No one saw Talia rush to check on Albert or Beverly lift the cage door off its hinges. The thing was heavy. Almost too heavy for her to carry but seeing her husband struggling for his life gave her all the additional motivation she required. Walking across the raised canvas platform, all she had to do on the other side was drop it.

Roy's injured shoulder screamed in agony, but Bruno's good hand was around his throat, and he knew he was fighting to stay alive. Little spots of light were beginning to dance in front of his eyes as the henchman cut off the blood supply to his brain, so it was with great surprise that Roy's opponent abruptly disappeared.

Roy followed the clanging sound, looking down to find Bruno sprawled across the floor again. He wore a cage door on his face.

Roy was about to look around when Beverly leapt from the canvas platform, her feet out and her teeth bared. The ninja kick she delivered to Thomas' jaw wouldn't exactly rival one performed by Jean Claude Van Damme. But it did the trick, bowling the second henchman back and away from Mila who once again took control of her gun.

Bouncing off the floor and getting back to her feet just as swiftly, Beverly said, "Hey, sweetie," and gave Roy a quick kiss. "Albert's hurt. I think he might need an ambulance."

Bewildered, Roy looked down at the cage door, across to the now empty cage, up at the platform from which his nearly eighty-year-old wife had just leapt and performed the entire routine again, his mouth opening and closing like a fish stranded on land.

After a few seconds, he manged to mumble, "How?"

A groan from Albert pulled their attention his way, Mila risking only the swiftest of glances to see what was happening.

"Is he okay?" she asked.

Beverly and Roy were clambering back onto the canvas to get to him, but it was Albert who answered.

"Not really. I've been perforated. I feel like a teabag." Talia had his head cradled in her arms.

"You look like one, old boy," said Roy, kneeling next to his friend.

"Oh, Albert," cried Beverly. "Can you sit up?"

With Talia's help, Albert levered his top half back to upright. Blood streamed from his cuts, coating his skin and staining his trousers.

Beverly put a brave face on it, but the blood loss concerned her. There was far too much of it.

"Where's his shirt?" she asked, looking around for anything she could use as a bandage.

Mila took a step to her left and snagged it. Unwilling to take her eyes off Thomas and Bruno, even though neither man looked ready to try anything, she held it out for Roy to take.

He removed his own jacket, and then his shirt, ripping the sleeves off so Beverly could use those as well.

Albert winced and gritted his teeth. His face had lost its colour, but he was alive. For now.

"We need to get him to a hospital," said Beverly, not knowing how they were going to achieve such a task. Her car was outside, but carrying Albert was beyond them.

Albert gripped her shoulder and wheezed, "Rex? Where's Rex?"

They all turned their eyes to the floor.

Frowning deeply, Roy asked, "Where are any of the dogs?"

Chapter 34

Rex ran.

The panther was behind him and only the head start he stole was keeping them apart. Unfortunately, he had no idea where he was going. The underground bunker system was a labyrinth of wide concrete corridors linking rooms of all sizes. He ran through some and past others, their closed doors hiding what might lay beyond. Would it be a way out or a dead end?

With no way to know, and unable to open the doors, Rex kept his head down and ran on.

"*Slow down, little dog*," the panther taunted. "*I want to play with you.*" The laugh that followed chilled Rex's spine.

Beginning to tire and panting hard, his tongue flapping from the left side of his mouth like a wet, pink flag, Rex could feel tendrils of panic stealing his confidence. He'd been running for a couple of minutes, but the panther remained hot on his heels.

A tight turn here, a set of stairs there, nothing was going to shake the sleek black cat. Not that such tactics would have worked on him had he been the one giving chase, but he would have used his nose. Cats weren't known for tracking, but that didn't matter because he'd never been more than a few yards ahead.

"*Keep running, little doggy.*" The panther laughed. "*There's nowhere to go.*"

The same thought had gone through Rex's mind more than once. How was he going to get out? What would happen if he did? In the open, he couldn't go any faster and the cat had already proved he could catch him in a straight race.

Abruptly, all those questions ended. He'd run out of places to go.

"*Whoops,*" said the panther.

Rex skidded to a stop. The latest corridor had led him into a large room, the dimensions not too dissimilar to the war room in which they started their chase. This room, however, held machinery. Rex couldn't know it, but he'd reached the bowels of the bunker system and the engineering sector where the air purification equipment and generators were installed.

Bulky machines lined the walls. Had they been installed in the middle of the floor he might have been able to run around them. With the panther still giving chase he could have emerged heading back the way he came. As it was, he could see gaps between the machines, but feared venturing down them would strand him in a narrow passageway.

Turning around, he faced the cat, and a small, sad laugh escaped his lips.

"*What's so funny?*" Raven growled.

Backing away and watching for the panther to launch his final attack, Rex mused on his fate. Of all the ways he could go out, getting killed by a cat, albeit one that was bigger than him, had never entered his head as a possibility. Yet here he was. He would fight. He would bite and rip and do his best, but he was no match for the powerful predator, and he knew it.

When Rex didn't answer, Raven stalked forward. "*I believe the humans call this a dead end.*"

"*How fitting.*"

"*For you, yes,*" growled the panther.

Rex's backend hit the front face of a large machine, and he stopped.

Raven stopped too. Facing the German Shepherd, it angered him that the dog showed almost no sign of fear. He ought to be quivering, but he stood firm, his eyes alert and looking for the inevitable attack to come.

Knowing it would make no difference what strategy the dog might have in his head, Raven slowly bunched the muscles in his back legs. This was going to be fun and when he was finished, he would find Cerberus and Hades. They needed to be taught a lesson too. The kind that ended with at least one of them very much dead.

Rex tried to control his breathing. His heart was maxed out from running and the adrenalin channelling through his body was only making it worse. Seeing the panther getting ready to leap, he prepared to jump out of the way. If he timed it right, the panther would miss him and smash into the machine. It was a slim chance, but the only tactic he could come up with.

Barely daring to breathe, Rex felt his forehead creasing when he noticed the panther was no longer looking at him. The cat's gaze had shifted to focus on something above his head. It was a trick. It had to be. The old 'look behind you' ruse to make him take his eyes off his opponent.

Well, he wasn't falling for it.

But the panther's eyes were moving now. Tracking upward, the black cat's head lifted.

Rex had no clue what was happening, but when the panther suddenly shot to the left, running after something Rex couldn't see, all he could do was watch. He knew he was supposed to be running away. With the panther distracted, the way out was suddenly clear, but what the heck was going on?

Raven's tail twitched and his back end wiggled with excitement in the moment before he pounced. Leaping at something unseen, he landed with his front paws leading, jubilantly trapping something beneath them.

Rex took a tentative step to his right, putting distance between himself and the panther.

Raven lifted his paws, his victorious grin suddenly crestfallen. Until his head snapped up and to the left.

Bewildered, Rex watched the black cat zip away again.

He knew he ought to be making his escape while the panther endured whatever was behind his psychotic break, but forcing his paws to move he couldn't help but watch the cat dart this way and that, grabbing at …

Wait.

There was a dot of red light.

Angling his eyes up, Rex needed only a second to see its source. Cerberus grinned down at him, his mouth open and his tongue lolling out. Rex could see the Doberman was fighting to stay quiet when he wanted to laugh out loud.

Next to him, lying on a raised walkway so his front paws and head dangled over the side, Hades held a laser pointer in his mouth.

"*Go!*" mouthed Cerberus, urging Rex to get moving with his eyes and his body language.

It was all the encouragement Rex needed. Slowly, but with his pace building once he was out of the maintenance room, Rex ran to get back to the humans.

Halfway there, the sound of paws on concrete caused him to slow until the Dobermans came into sight.

"*Ha! We got him good,*" laughed Hades. He was limping and Rex could see traces of blood matted into his fur, but whatever injuries he'd sustained would be recoverable.

Jogging together, Rex's pace slower so they wouldn't leave Hades behind, he asked, "*How did you know to do that?*"

"*The red light?*" Cerberus asked. "*We saw the mayor doing it once. Raven can't resist it. The thing drives him nuts. It's like he's hypnotised by it.*"

"*Where is it now?*"

"*Left it there,*" said Hades. "*It's pointing at a wall a few feet above Raven's reach. Last we saw he was jumping to get it. I expect he'll be there until the battery runs out.*"

Rex expressed his gratitude and acknowledged that he'd helped them first by attacking Raven when he was biting Hades. Together, the three dogs made their way back through the maze of tunnels, only stopping when they heard humans arguing.

Rex sniffed the air. "*That's not my human. That's ...*"

"*The mayor and Sabrina,*" grinned Hades.

Chapter 35

Albert was back on his feet, though he wasn't exactly moving under his own steam. Roy and Beverly were either side of him, supporting his weight. That he was in poor shape was not in question. Whether he would live through the night was, but no one wanted to discuss his odds aloud.

Unable to find anything to tie Bruno and Thomas up with, Mila and Talia forced them into the cage. It required a few deliberate near miss shots to convince them the sisters weren't bluffing, and the two men barely fit through the opening. But they went in, the door was refitted, and the padlock secured them.

Beverly located the split pin – she'd dropped it when she clambered out of the cage – and made a show of tucking it into a pocket.

One less problem to worry about, all five aimed their feet back toward the entrance. They retraced their steps, hoping they were getting it right in the confusing rabbit warren of crisscrossing passageways.

Roy thought he ought to be able to lead them, but the decades since he was last in the bunker complex meant he was no more familiar with it than anyone else.

Coming to the first set of stairs, they heard the voices.

Straining her hearing, Talia said, "That's …"

"The mayor and Sabrina," said Albert, finishing her sentence.

Surprised to hear him speak, Roy had thought his friend to be barely conscious, he asked, "You still with us, old boy?"

Albert, slowly and with a wince of pain, removed his arms from around his neighbours' shoulders.

"For now, at least. I can't say I'm up to doing much, but I think perhaps we should finish this game." The sisters were armed, and he doubted Horst and Sabrina were. Oh, the mayor probably had his sword still, but that wasn't worth much in a gunfight.

"Come on," he grumbled. "I think we can all guess where they are."

They found Sabrina in the server room. She was on the ground, her hands pressed tight to her abdomen where blood seeped between her fingers.

"He skewered me," she wheezed. "We were supposed to be partners." A tear rolled down her right cheek but whether it was from the pain, or from the realisation her latest criminal enterprise was about to fail, Albert couldn't tell.

He wanted to condemn her, but right now she was a woman in trouble, and she would die if they didn't help her.

With Beverly checking her wounds, Albert asked, "Which way did he go?"

Sabrina grunted, sucking in a hard breath when an attempt to shift position sent a wave of pain through her. Falling to one side until Beverly caught her, she managed to hiss, "He transferred everything to a Swiss bank account and left. You'll never catch him."

Albert might have argued, but a sound from the vicinity of the server room door yanked his attention around.

Rex was coming through it and having seen his human, he was bounding across the floor to get to him.

In danger of being knocked down by his dog's enthusiasm, Albert shouted, "Whoa, boy!"

"It's the Dobermans!" yelled Mila, swinging her gun around to aim at the dogs who chased her through the woods. She was convinced they would have ripped her apart if they'd been able to catch her.

"*They're with me!*" Rex barked. "*Don't shoot them!*"

Mercifully, Mila didn't pull the trigger, but it wasn't Rex's plea that stopped her, but the way the black and tan dogs behaved. Unlike every other time she'd seen them, they weren't acting aggressively, and she remembered how they attacked Bruno and Thomas.

Racing to get to Albert, Rex managed to skid to a stop just in time. He could smell the old man's blood and didn't like how much of it he could see. He looked deathly pale, too.

Rex licked and nuzzled Albert's hands, letting his human ruffle and scratch the fur around his neck.

"All right, Rex. All right. I'm going to be okay." Albert hoped that was true, but he was beginning to feel quite faint again. Slowly lowering himself down to one knee, Albert took Rex's face in both hands. "I have a task for you, Rex."

Rex stopped his tail from wagging and listened.

"You know the man I was fighting? The one they call 'the mayor'? Can you find his scent?"

Rex's body was ramrod straight and so still it was hard to tell he wasn't stuffed. "*It is time for chase and bite?*" he asked, hoping he was about to receive a command he adored above all others.

"Rex, my glorious dog," Albert rose back to full height on wobbly knees and pointed to the door. "Sic 'em."

Bolting for the door, Rex yelled, "*Come on!*" at Cerberus and Hades, zipping between them with such haste and determination they were almost pulled off their paws by the vacuum he left behind.

"We should leave, too," Albert said, looking for Roy to support him again.

Talia looked down at Sabrina. "What about her?"

Beverly said, "She can't be moved. Not by us at least. If we can find help, we'll send it to her."

Sabrina offered no argument and watched them leave without comment.

Retracing their steps again, Albert and his friends found their way to the exit. The door was open, a good thing because it had allowed the dogs to continue their pursuit.

Running outside, the humans were shocked to find the storm had passed. Rainwater coated the ground, and they could hear it dripping from the trees and running down the drainpipes, but the sky above now showed patches of clear where the stars shone through.

However, while escape from the bunker complex had been easier than expected, the sound of approaching sirens promised a new complication.

"Oh, no," wailed Beverly. "It's the police!"

Mila huffed, "Horst must have called them when he saw us getting the upper hand."

With the police in his pocket, the mayor would be able to make their bodies disappear and the enormous former military base offered so much land their burial spots would never be found.

"Quick, my love!" Roy pushed Beverly to get moving. "The car!"

"I don't have the keys!" she wailed, hurrying to get to it all the same.

"Then we'd better hope they are in it!"

Headlights swept toward them, half a dozen cars zooming through the compound. The gates at the entrance were wide open, the guards there undoubtedly letting them through with a wave and a smile.

"Keys!" Beverly exclaimed, relieved to find them in the car's ignition.

Moving as fast as they could, Mila and Talia bundled Albert into the backseat, wedging his sagging body between theirs. The moment Roy's butt hit his seat, Beverly stomped on the gas, propelling the car forward in a slew of gravel.

Roy's door slammed shut and he fought to find his seatbelt.

"Where are you going, woman?" he questioned, shouting to be heard above the roaring engine.

"Away!" Beverly screamed back at him.

Seeing the BMW's fleeing taillights some of the police gave chase, but not all of them. Two cars stayed on Beverly's tail while the rest spread out. Some stopped outside the open door to the bunker complex, others peeled off to tackle the camp's residents who were stumbling from their accommodation looking dazed and afraid.

Staring through the back window and trying to hold on, Mila saw yet more police cars entering the base. They were trapped and getting clear was going to be tough. Yet it was life or death now. Getting caught was not an option and though it chilled her blood, she knew she might have to shoot her way to freedom.

Beverly hooked a hard right at the end of a tall building, the backend skidding across the surface of the road. In the back, Albert and the sisters were thrown to one side and then the other as forces corrected themselves.

Roy's wife was driving like a mad woman, but the cops were catching her. Their skills outmatched hers and their cars didn't contain nearly so many heavy humans.

"Rex?" Albert muttered incoherently. "Where's Rex?"

Chapter 36

"*This way*," Rex confirmed.

When they left the underground bunker, it took a few moments to find the mayor's scent and to be sure which way he went. Concerned he might have found a car and be far, far away already, Rex was delighted to track his smell across the camp to the headquarters building.

Getting inside proved a challenge, but only until they worked out that the front door wasn't locked. It opened outward, and the handle was very much not designed to be operated by a dog's paw, but they found that if one of them jumped against the door, it would bounce just a little. A second dog had to wedge a paw or his muzzle into the gap and then use it to wiggle the door open.

It took three attempts to get the timing right, but they found their way inside.

Now the mayor's scent was everywhere. It was a building he occupied frequently, but it also wasn't that big. The mayor was here somewhere, and they could split up to search more swiftly.

Sending Cerberus left and Hades right, Rex chose the stairs. He remembered where to find the mayor's office and was surprised to not find him there. A cool breeze from outside blew in through an open window, carrying the sounds of the patrol car sirens and the squeal of their tyres as they raced through the camp's main entrance.

Rex was about to leave the mayor's office to search elsewhere when he caught a whisper of noise coming from the office's other door.

Rex wanted to bark to bring the other dogs to him, but doing so would alert the mayor who Rex could now hear coming closer.

Moments later, the door opened, the mayor striding through it to stop abruptly when he saw Albert's German Shepherd blocking his path.

Rex bared his teeth. "*You hurt my human. I love that old man, and you made him bleed. I think it only fair I return the gesture.*"

Horst Schultz had his arms filled with money. Since the very start, when he went looking for a partner and found Sabrina, he'd been converting a percentage of his cut into cash. Most of the money he made running the Bitcoin enterprise, which was not only above board but genuinely made money for its investors, went out of the country to a private bank account in the Cayman Islands, but Horst liked to think of himself as a prudent man. To that end, his escape plan, if it were to ever all go wrong, was to disappear with everything the Halvorsen Syndicate had invested with him at that time.

After Albert Smith cheated during their duel, employing gutter tactics when Horst expected him to honour their fight as a gentleman, Sabrina caught him transferring it all, including her cut, and went berserk. She believed Ulv 'the wolf' would find him no matter where he went and wanted no part of Horst's deception. In her opinion, you don't steal from gangsters unless you want to end up in little pieces.

He'd lusted after the beautiful Swedish woman for years without her once considering him to be a viable partner. So it was with a tinge of regret that he stuck her with his sword, but also a sense of righteous balance. Had she been his lover, it would never have happened.

Escaping the bunker, Horst knew he needed to make all haste to get away, but to vanish he needed cash and that was in the back room behind his office. He had almost six million Euros stashed in a cupboard, and he wasn't leaving without it.

Cursing himself for not thinking to purchase a bag it could go in, Horst grabbed as much as he could and was going to go back for the rest. But now he was facing an angry dog, so with his panther nowhere in sight, he dropped the lot and grabbed for his sword.

Rex growled. He knew what the weapon was. He'd seen what it did to his human, but he'd been given a command to 'sic em' and was going to see it through.

Chapter 37

The backend of the BMW swinging out again, Beverly drove faster than she had ever attempted before. The patrol cars were right on her, both looking for a way to get alongside. She'd expected them to start shooting and was surprised they hadn't yet.

On the backseat, Mila and Talia exchanged a glance. They had the guns still. If they shot at the police cars they would miss – the ride was just too bumpy and unpredictable for anything but blind luck to score a hit, but that was the only thing stopping them. Beverly couldn't shake their pursuers and sooner or later it was going to become a shootout.

Gripping the steering wheel so tight her knuckles were white, Beverly screamed, "Hold on! I'm going to try something!"

"Hold on?" questioned Roy in the passenger seat. "Are you kidding?" His grip on the handle above his head threatened to rip it free of its mounts and he had both legs and his other arm bracing against the dashboard and footwell to keep himself in place. Then his wife's words filtered through his terror-addled brain. "Wait. You're going to try something?"

Beverly didn't reply. She knew the camp well enough, having spent many years there when it was still an RAF base, and doubted the layout had changed all that much. Around the next corner, assuming nothing had changed, was the workshop where they serviced, maintained, and repaired the ground support vehicles. She knew about it because one of her friends got a job there as the secretary.

Rounding the corner, one wheel lifting off the road as the car fought against conflicting physics, she saw what she wanted.

Roy saw it too. "You're not going to …"

"Yes, I am!"

It was a Hail Mary play. Directly to their front a pair of giant concrete ramps led to an inspection platform. Beverly could recall seeing large vehicles sitting atop it with mechanics working underneath. In all likelihood she was about to crash, but if she didn't the car would balance on two wheels and sail through a narrow gap between two buildings to leave the cops behind. It could just be the chance they needed.

In the back seat, Mila saw what was about to happen. "Oh. My. Goooooddddd!"

The front left wheel hit the ramp to the right, closely followed by the back left wheel. The pitch of the ramp launched the car into the air but the wheels on the right hand side stayed on the ground. Just like that they were on two wheels and still doing sixty miles per hour.

Hanging on for dear life, Roy clung to his side of the car. With eyes bugging from his head, he saw the gap between the buildings. They were going to make it.

"We're going to make it!" he whooped, the incredibly reckless stunt looking like it might actually pay off.

Until they started to drift.

"Um." Roy held up a hand, using it to indicate where they ought to be going.

But it was too late, and they slammed into the side of a building, crumpling the front of the BMW and setting off the air bags. The car fell back to earth, landing with a bone-crunching crump. It bounced on the suspension a few times, the occupants all struggling to catch their breath.

The cop cars skidded to a stop, one either side of the car, the officers inside spilling out with their weapons drawn.

Sensing this was her last stand, Mila reached out to grab her sister's hand and when their fingers locked across the centre of the car, she pointed her gun out of the window. How she had arrived at a situation where she was about to shoot a cop she could not fathom.

"Wait," croaked Albert, challenging everyone's belief that he was unconscious. "Don't shoot. I think they're on our side."

Chapter 38

Rex growled. He was eight feet from his target, but the sword made any attack perilous.

"Get out of my way, dog," snarled the mayor. Cops were sweeping into the compound and that could only mean one thing: Albert had figured out enough to give Chief Kramer reason to dig further. Horst knew the wily old cop suspected something, but he'd always been able to keep him at arm's length.

Now, though … well, talking his way out was going to be a challenge. Chief Kramer wasn't the kind of man who would accept a bribe, even with the amount of money Horst could offer him.

For years they had worked hand in hand, but Horst always knew the chief of police only allowed him to use his officers so he could keep an eye on what the mayor was up to. That hadn't been a problem until now, but maybe the officers didn't know everything. Maybe they weren't here with implicit instructions to arrest him on sight.

If they didn't know, he would be able to get close enough to kill one. The sword would do the job and then he could take a patrol car. All he had to do was get out of the camp. After that, with the money he carried, he could buy his way out of the country.

Except the dog was in his way.

He took a menacing step forward, swinging the sword at the dog's head.

Rex backed away a pace. If he timed it right, he would be able to lunge and bite when the sword came past. Conversely, if he timed it wrong, he would die.

A savage smile splitting his lips, Horst took another step and swung the sword again. He was going to drive the dog back or he was going to kill him. He really didn't care which. Bending his knees, he scooped a few bundles of bank notes, stuffing them into his trouser pockets.

He forgot his shirt when he fled the bunker, and hadn't been able find anything to replace it. Naked from the waist up, his skin shone with sweat despite the cold and there were smears of dirt coating it where he'd rolled on the floor.

"*Need some help here?*" asked Hades, coming through the door behind Rex.

Cerberus was right behind him. "*I think it's about time we showed this human what it's like to be part of a pack.*"

The mayor's face fell.

The dogs bared their teeth again and took a collective step forward.

Horst believed he could get one dog easily enough, but the moment he did the other two would be on him. He needed only a split second to weigh his options and decide. Bolting, he spun off one foot and ran. Heading for the door at the back of his office, Cerberus got there first.

Cut off, Horst changed direction. The dogs were barking, and to his ears it sounded like they were communicating. With a jolt, he saw they had herded him. He was running toward the windows and there was nowhere else for him to go.

He knew he wasn't in the best shape of his life. Far from it, in fact, but he was only one floor up. The fall was thirty feet or so, and entirely survivable. At the open window, he vaulted, placing one hand on the open sill and leaping into free air.

Six cops watched the mayor of Hoffenholen fall. They were just getting out of their cars. The guards on the front gate had surrendered without a fuss when they saw the barrage of weapons pointing their way, and the rest of the guards were being rounded up.

From the radio, they knew some of their colleagues had found an injured woman in the warren of underground bunkers. Bizarrely, the report was that she'd been run through with a sword and right before their eyes, the mayor plummeted earthwards with bank notes trailing behind him like raining confetti and a sword gripped tightly in his right hand.

One nudged another. "He looks a little like *Bruce Willis* in *Die Hard*."

"Oh, yeah. In that scene where he jumps off the top of *Nakatomi Plaza*."

"Yeah. That's it. Except he forgot to tie the firehose around his waist."

To accentuate the point, the mayor landed on his feet with a crunch that could be heard across the compound. Both his legs snapped, the bones in his ankles shattering along with his tibias and fibulas.

His howl reached the dogs' ears when all three appeared in the window above. They looked down on the fallen, flailing figure.

"*Anyone feel like signing their name on him?*" Rex asked, ducking back and running for the door.

Hades looked at Cerberus. "*Sign our names?*"

Chapter 39

Chief Kramer approached the wounded BMW with his sidearm still in its holster. He kept his arms out to his sides and made sure his hands were obviously empty.

"Put your guns away," he ordered his officers.

Twisting to look, Beverly asked, "What's happening? Albert, what did you mean they are on our side?"

Feeling spent, Albert was slumped on the backseat, but he was conscious and able to reply. "I thought Chief Kramer was warning me off when he came to visit me and he was, but for my own good, not on behalf of the mayor."

"How do you know that?" asked Mila, her right index finger still hovering over the trigger.

"Do you recall the mayor calling us on Beverly's phone? When he did that, he told me not to alert the police."

"My word," gasped Roy. "He did, didn't he!"

"I'd been wondering about it for a while. There were things he said that first time we spoke."

Chief Kramer appeared at Beverly's door where he crouched a little to look inside.

"Everyone okay?" he asked.

"No," said Roy. "Albert's hurt. That crazy mayor of yours made him fight a duel with a sword. He's lost a lot of blood."

"Ambulances are on their way," the chief of police replied, swinging his gaze to the backseat. "Can I ask that you surrender those weapons, please."

Flooded with relief, Mila and Talia handed them over, stepping from the car on shaky legs.

The radios crackled, the message about the mayor jumping from the headquarters building reaching every set of ears.

"Less than he deserves," snapped Beverly, looking down at her ruined car.

"Oh, I think he'll get the rest of it when he goes before a judge," said Chief Kramer.

They helped Albert into the back of the chief's car, Beverly, Roy, and the sisters all taking spaces in the two patrol cars so they could return to the front of the camp where all the action was taking place.

The chief needed to be there to control it.

Despite his discomfort and the faintness he felt from the loss of blood, Albert couldn't help cracking a smile when the radio crackled again and a voice reported that the mayor was now soaked.

"Soaked?" questioned Chief Kramer. "Did someone set a firehose on him?"

Albert choked, a cackle of laughter bursting from him even though it hurt so much to do so.

Collapsing back into the fabric of his chair, he said, "Well done, Rex. Well done."

Chapter 40

The following morning, sitting in his hospital bed, Albert was pleased to see Chief Kramer approaching. When he opened his door to let Rex inside, he was overcome with joy.

So too was Rex, who bounded across the room to land with his front paws on the bed.

The doctor already in the room frowned deeply, but didn't say anything.

Ruffling his fur, Albert fussed his dog.

His injuries were stitched and would heal. The cut to his right bicep was the worst. It made his arm hard to use, but that too would heal in time. He was no longer considered to be in any danger, and they were already threatening to let him go.

All three of his children had visited that morning. They were staying in local accommodation, getting a little rest after dropping everything and driving through the night to get to him. They would take him home when the doctor said they could. Albert's adventures were over. For a short while at least and he presented no argument. He needed to take some time to recover, and it was nearly Christmas, after all.

When Thomas and Bruno burst in on them at their hotel room, Albert had pressed the button on his phone to reconnect his son. It was a long shot, but Albert knew if his son heard the mayor's henchmen taking them, he would swing into action. Gary said they needed something actionable to move against the Unlimited Horizons camp and what better than a kidnapping?

Gary needed almost no time at all to identify the local police chief his father admitted annoying and everything proceeded from there. Europol wanted to coordinate an assault on the compound, but Chief Kramer refused to wait. It was a live situation, and he took the initiative, operating on the word of a detective superintendent from London who he didn't know and had no good reason to trust.

Had Gary not been Albert's son, Chief Kramer wouldn't have risked his entire career. Albert was very glad he had.

"You know," said Chief Kramer, "I genuinely expected you to leave after I warned you to back off. I had an officer working undercover and would have brought the operation down in time."

"Did you know what was going on?"

Chief Kramer gave a sad shake of his head. "No. Not really. I was certain there was something. The mayor funded his own political campaigns and claimed the money all came from investments."

"Well, it did, I guess."

"Yes, investments made by criminals. Europol won't let me anywhere near it, but that's okay. I don't have to worry about the rest of the world. My business is here in Hoffenholen."

"I thought for a while that you were working with him," Albert admitted.

"Yes, I wanted to give you that impression. Again, I worried you were going to get yourself into trouble and it's my job to keep the civilian population safe. I thought that if you believed you were up against the local police as well, you might choose to back off from your investigation."

Albert shrugged. "I never was particularly bright."

They chatted for a while, the chief of police bringing Albert up to date on developments over the last few hours. The residents staying under the care of Unlimited Horizons were still there. The infrastructure underpinning the mayor's Bitcoin money laundering operation was genuine. Spiritual guidance counsellor Stefan had no clue there was anything else going on. That the operation was funded by money illegally gained and traded meant the facility would soon be shut down, but the residents were seen as victims too and were being treated accordingly.

The board members of Digital Ascensions Investments were all found to be residents in the Unlimited Horizons community. They all claimed to have no clue their names, and in some cases also faces, were being used to front the cryptocurrency platform, but were under investigation anyway.

Sabrina survived her injury and was elsewhere in the hospital where she would recover under armed guard. Her future involved a small cell in a big jail.

Mayor Horst Schultz was not going to win his re-election campaign. No one in the town of Hoffenholen cared all that much. His broken bones had been reset during the night and much like Sabrina, he was going to be convicted.

Europol agents had arrived after Albert left the camp in the back of an ambulance. Their lead agent swiftly seized control of the case, shutting Chief Kramer out while simultaneously commandeering some of his officers. Chief Kramer was tight-lipped on the subject, but Albert knew it would annoy the local man.

The chief had other duties to which he had to attend, but as he made ready to depart, two different faces appeared in the hallway outside his room.

"Albert!" cried Mila, excited to see him sitting up. "And Rex." She made a big fuss of the dog before settling into a seat next to Albert's bed.

Talia had less to say. She only knew Albert through her sister but understood how much she owed the elderly man.

The sisters were returning to Belarus and were set to depart later that day. They had enough money to support themselves for the time being and a promise from Europol that the money Unlimited Horizons took would be returned when they finally figured out who should have what. Naturally, the cash in Horst's possession had been seized, but the agents were after the bigger fish.

It would take time to prove where the money came from, but the team of law enforcement officers were determined to bring down the Halvorsen Syndicate.

When Mila bade Albert a tearful goodbye, hugging him as tightly as she could without hurting him, she did so just as his next visitor arrived. This time it was his youngest son, Randall.

"There's a small army of reporters outside the hospital," he reported. "A chap called Dieter stopped me. He's hoping for an exclusive interview. I assume you'll be wanting to go out the back way."

"No," Albert grumbled, trying to change position without wincing too much. "I owe them." He couldn't claim to be happy about it, but he'd deceived them in his first bid to rescue Talia, so it was only fair he acquiesced to their requests now.

"Are they letting you out?" Randall asked.

Albert looked at the doctor.

He nodded. "Yes. There's no reason to keep you, but please do take it slow the next few weeks. We replaced the blood you lost but your body will work overtime to repair the damage, and you will be weaker than normal." He paused next to the door. "I'll have your discharge paperwork made out."

"Did you hear that, Rex? We can go home. I think I quite fancy a rest, truth be told."

Randall scoffed, "You're going to take a rest? That would be new."

Epilogue

Alexander Halvorsen looked out through the window of his Norrkoping Penthouse suite. He was yet to find out what exactly had happened, but it appeared that the police, aided by international law enforcement agencies, had raided a facility in Germany where a fat chunk of his money was laundered each year.

The accountant who delivered the bad news less than an hour earlier was already at the bottom of the Baltic Sea.

The sum he'd lost wouldn't impact his operation too badly, though it was more than the gross domestic product of many small nations. What stung most was the exposure. Law enforcement agencies would be able to trace the money back to him.

The cryptocurrency system kept it invisible, but now they were on the inside, the police would be able to unpick the layers of security, their forensic accountants undoubtedly smart enough to find the origin point.

Horst Schultz, a name he knew only through his sister, would meet a sticky end before he could stand trial, as would the woman who his sister once shared a cell with. It was she who brought the German politician into it.

They didn't concern him. So far as 'the wolf' was concerned, they were already taken care of. What did bother him was the man he had just watched on the evening news. Like most people, Alexander had to be reminded why he recognised the name, but having heard the reporter talking, it all came back to him.

Albert Smith was an old man from England who stumbled upon a mystery involving a distant member of the British royal family and ended up making himself famous. There ought to be no reason why their paths would ever cross, but the ageing sleuth didn't know when to stop sticking his nose where it wasn't wanted and this time …

"This time," Alexander remarked to himself, "it will cost you your life."

The End

Author notes:

Hello, Dear Reader,

Thank you for reading all the way to the end of this story and beyond. I shall assume you enjoyed it since you got this far. I use my author notes section to talk a little about elements of the story that might require some explanation, and to share with you what was going on in my life at the time of writing.

The latter element is so that, many years from now, a new reader might follow through the library of books I have produced (more than one hundred in the eight years since the first one) and observe the transition from soldier to corporate lacky, and finally to full time author, and husband to father to (hopefully) grandparent.

I served in Germany for the majority of my military career, although to make that claim I must ignore all the times when I wasn't there. While nominally my post was in Germany, I was in Bosnia, or Iraq, or wherever else they thought it might be fun to send me.

Nevertheless, I feel like I spent a lot of my life in the middle of Europe and regret not getting out to explore it more. A combination of too little expendable income, spending my evenings and weekends studying, and that youthful trait for thinking there would always be time to do those things later, meant I rarely left the camp when there was so much beyond it to explore.

I cannot say whether 'Schnellie' is a term used outside of the British military living in Germany, but it was a universal term for any place selling food to take away. It is derived from the word 'Schnell' which means fast or swift. I remember the ones I frequented very well.

When I started writing this book, my four-year-old daughter, Hermione, had just returned home from a stay in a children's hospital in London. There she had a feeding tube fitted to her stomach. She is autistic and has a sensory processing disorder that affects her food decisions. Her dislike, or possibly distrust, of certain textures dictates that she rejects almost everything we try to feed her. Years of fighting with paediatricians and dieticians resulted in nothing until her vitamins deficiencies robbed her eyesight.

At four she is blind and though it is possible that her eyesight will return now that her vitamin levels have been addressed, there is no guarantee she will ever see again.

As you might imagine, this is a nightmare for me as a parent and were she not so able to adapt and seem so continuously happy, I would be struggling far more than I am. My productivity is a fraction of what it was, but my little girl will always take priority.

This book is the first one I have ever had to put to one side because I couldn't figure out how to make the story work. I am a discovery writer, which means I figure out the details as I go. Sometimes, that means I have to rewrite a big chunk when I decide halfway through to change something important at the start, but often as not I lay the track as I run along it and arrive at the end without too much bother.

The issue with this one was the motivation behind Mila's infiltration of the camp and what they were doing beneath the cover it gave. Mila was almost an undercover cop, but I couldn't make that work. The camp was almost a staging point for illegal immigration into the UK (a major political headache here if you are not aware). In the end, I'm content the story is right, and I'm really happy with the changes I made.

Hopefully, I found the right blend of humour, action, and emotion.

Having started this book in January, I have written three other titles before finally getting to the end of this one. It is now the back end of May, and I am going on vacation in less than forty hours. I have been cutting my sleep to get this finished so it won't plague my brain while I'm supposed to be playing with my kids.

The next Albert Smith adventure will bring back an old adversary and return to a storyline started in the second book. We are heading to a crescendo at the end of the series where our plucky duo will face off against multiple enemies. It is going to be fun to write.

However, the next book on my list to craft is the final book in my Felicity Philips series and both Rex and Albert will appear in it. They are attending a royal wedding in Canterbury Cathedral. If you have already read the previous series, you will know how that came about.

Take care.

Steve Higgs

History of the dish:

A uthor's note: Admittedly, I messed up with this dish because Wiener Schnitzels are Austrian not German, but they are also delicious so I decided to keep things as they are.

Wiener Schnitzel, which translates to "Viennese cutlet" in English, is a traditional Austrian dish that consists of a thinly sliced veal cutlet that is breaded and fried to golden brown perfection. The dish is typically served with a squeeze of lemon and a side of potatoes, salad, or cucumber slices. The origins of Wiener Schnitzel date back to the 18th century, when it was served as a luxury dish in the royal courts of Vienna. Over time, the dish gained popularity and spread throughout Austria, becoming a staple of the country's cuisine.

The history of Wiener Schnitzel is a fascinating story that involves the culinary traditions of Austria and the cultural exchange between European countries. The dish is believed to have come about when Austrian chefs were inspired by the Italian dish "cotoletta alla milanese," which consists of a breaded and fried veal cutlet. The Austrian chefs adapted the recipe to their own tastes, using veal instead of pork and adding their own unique twist to the breading and frying process.

Over the centuries, Wiener Schnitzel has undergone significant changes, with various regions in Austria developing their own unique variations of the dish. In Vienna, the traditional Wiener Schnitzel is made with veal, while in other parts of the country, pork or chicken may be used as a substitute. The breading and frying process has also evolved, with some recipes calling for a light dusting of flour, while others require a thicker coating of breadcrumbs.

Check below for the recipe and have fun making this for yourself.

Weiner Schnitzel Recipe

Ingredients:

- 1 ½ pounds veal cutlets
- ½ cup all-purpose flour
- 2 large eggs
- 3 tablespoons grated Parmesan cheese
- 2 tablespoons milk
- 1 teaspoon minced parsley
- ½ teaspoon salt
- ¼ teaspoon pepper
- 1 pinch ground nutmeg
- 1 cup dry breadcrumbs
- 6 tablespoons butter
- 4 slices lemon

Directions:

1. Place veal cutlets between 2 sheets of heavy plastic on a solid, level surface. Firmly pound cutlets with the smooth side of a meat mallet to a 1/4-inch thickness. Dip cutlets in flour to coat; shake off excess.

2. Beat eggs, Parmesan cheese, milk, parsley, salt, pepper, and nutmeg together in a shallow bowl until combined. Place breadcrumbs on a plate.

3. Dip each cutlet into the egg mixture, then press in breadcrumbs to coat. Place coated cutlets on a plate and refrigerate for 1 hour to overnight.

4. Melt butter in a large skillet over medium heat. Cook breaded cutlets in butter until browned, about 3 minutes per side. Transfer cutlets to a serving platter and pour pan juices over them. Garnish with lemon slices.

What's Next for Albert and Rex?

Convalescing after his recent injuries, Albert Smith is taking it easy ... until a face from his past appears on his TV screen and everything changes.

There's an old score to settle and this time his quest for justice will take him from his quiet English home to the foot of the Alps.

With Rex faithfully at his side, they hunt for a criminal no one else on the planet even knows exists.

You see, it's all about gold. A dangerous word too many people have killed and died for. There is treasure in the ground, buried more than eighty years ago by a man the Nazis entrusted to ship their plunder back to Berlin.

The people looking for it will do anything to protect their secret. Even kill.

So when an old man and his dog come nosing around ... well, let's just say things are going to get deadly.

Free Books and More

Want to see what else I have written? Go to my website.

https://stevehiggsbooks.com/

Or sign up to my newsletter where you will get sneak peaks, exclusive giveaways, behind the scenes content, and more. Plus, you'll be notified of Fan Pricing events when they occur and get exclusive offers from other authors because all UF writers are automatically friends.

https://stevehiggsbooks.com/newsletter/

Prefer social media? Join my thriving Facebook community.

Want to join the inner circle where you can keep up to date with everything? This is a free group on Facebook where you can hang out with likeminded individuals and enjoy discussing my books. There is cake too (but only if you bring it).

https://www.facebook.com/groups/1151907108277718

Printed in Dunstable, United Kingdom